More Books by Miriam Auerbach from Bell Bridge Books

The Dirty Harriet Mystery Series

Dead in Boca
Book 3

Dirty Harriet Rides Again
Book 2

Dirty Harriet
Book 1

Boca Undercover

Book 4 in the Dirty Harriet Mystery Series

by

Miriam Auerbach

To Prudy,
With Best Wishes,

Miriam Auerbach

Bell Bridge Books

Bell Bridge Books
PO BOX 300921
Memphis, TN 38130
Print ISBN: 978-1-61194-558-4

Bell Bridge Books is an Imprint of BelleBooks, Inc.

Copyright © 2014 by Miriam Auerbach

Printed and bound in the United States of America.

We at BelleBooks enjoy hearing from readers.
Visit our websites
BelleBooks.com
BellBridgeBooks.com
ImaJinnBooks.com

10 9 8 7 6 5 4 3 2 1

Cover design: Debra Dixon
Interior design: Hank Smith
Photo/Art credits:
Graphic background (manipulated) © Les Cunliffe | Dreamstime.com
Woman (manipulated) © Branislav Ostojic | Dreamstime.com
Bullet holes (manipulated) © Robert Adrian Hillman | Dreamstime.com
Ocean view (manipulated) © 13claudio13 | Dreamstime.com

:Lubh:01:

Dedication

To David Rafaidus
Superhusband

Chapter 1

IT IS A TRUTH universally acknowledged that a single woman in possession of a good boob job must be on the hunt for a husband. The known universe, in this case, is brassy, ritzy Boca Raton, Florida, a place where the personal power plays make those in Jane Austen's universe, or for that matter, the Real Housewives of New Jersey, look like amateur hour.

Our huntress is one Brigitta "Gitta" Larsen O'Malley Castellano, a.k.a. the "Danish Dish." She's a twice-widowed former Miss Denmark and third-runner up for Miss Universe 1992. Our prey is one Kevin Reilly. More on him later. And your humble social chronicler of their little comedy of mismanners is I, Harriet Horowitz, formerly a member of Gitta's tribe of Boca Babes, now a swamp-dwelling motorcycle maven.

But this story is not all about mating maneuvers, misunderstood men, and meddling mothers. It's about murder. Or so, at least, Gitta insisted when she called me in hysterics one fine October Sunday afternoon as I was polishing my Harley Hugger on the front porch of my log cabin in the Everglades west of Boca. I was enjoying the seventy-five degree, low-humidity air—a long-awaited respite from a languid, hot summer that had culminated in a hurricane.

The caller ID on my cell read "The Oasis," so I knew it had to be Gitta. She had checked herself into that resort spa/drug rehab facility for the rich and famous two weeks previously. The reason: Gitta was a cokehead . . . and Reilly was a cop. No, he hadn't busted her; they'd met when he caught the case of the murder of her second spouse, "Junior" Castellano, who was actually her senior by a good twenty-five years. Can you say "trophy wife?" If so, you've already got the inside line on what makes the Boca universe spin.

Now, however, Gitta was climbing down the marriage ladder, setting her sights on Reilly, whose salary as a Boca Raton P.D. detective was laughable by Boca Babe standards. But Gitta had decided that after decades of molding herself to the desires of wealthy, older men, she now wanted a relationship based on authenticity. And I guess you couldn't be authentic if you were addicted.

Hell, I should know—I too had been an addict. An addict to the Life of Luxury. Which ended when I blew away my rich but abusive husband, Bruce Barfknecht. In self-defense. Now, as far as I was concerned, you couldn't be more authentic than when dominating a five-hundred pound machine hurtling down an open road at eighty miles an hour. It's no coincidence that motorcycle experiences—whether riding or repair—have been compared to Zen. Both practices propel you into an alternate reality where you're in communion with . . . well, I don't know what, but something beyond yourself.

Gitta's call snatched me out of my biker bliss and back to Boca bizarreness.

"Harriet!" she rasped. "Help me!"

"What's wrong, Gitta?" I asked with a good deal of wariness. Her coming to me for help couldn't bear any positive implications. I mean, it's not like we were BFFs or anything. Back in the day, we'd been compatriots in conspicuous consumption, spending our days in boutique shops and beauty salons. But leaving my Life of Luxury in the dust in order to recover from my addiction had meant leaving all my faux friends, like Gitta, too. For their part, they'd been all too happy to distance themselves from me—the woman who had very publicly shattered the illusion of Boca perfection that they worked so hard to maintain. It was only in the last few months that circumstances had led me and Gitta to re-establish our acquaintance.

And those circumstances were hardly happy ones. The last time Gitta had asked for my help—in finding Junior's killer—I'd been sucked into a moral sinkhole so deep I still struggled, at times, with the repercussions. So you can see why I was on my guard.

Which turned to outright disgust when Gitta whispered, "They're killing people in here."

I know paranoia when I hear it. Especially the cocaine-induced variety. Bruce had evidenced the same symptoms—right up until I grabbed the .44 Magnum he'd taken to carrying and shot him with it as he was about to pound me with his fists. Again.

The coke might have left Gitta's body since she'd been in rehab, but apparently her brain hadn't gotten the memo. It was still operating in madness mode. Yet it had its own internal logic: if people were being killed at The Oasis, that would be a great reason for Gitta to get the hell out of there. And resume her habit. Which, honestly, I didn't want to happen. Despite my distrust of her, I had to give her credit for wanting to change her life. And beyond that, I had discovered, over the past few years of my own recovery, that part of maintaining my own sanity meant helping others.

"Gitta," I said, "I'm sure you're safe. You're where you need to be right now."

"No!" she said with panicked urgency. "You have to believe me!"

"Why don't you take a deep breath and, uh, get a massage or something?" I figured the place operated like an all-inclusive vacation. Minus the martinis and mai-tais, of course. "I'm sure you'll feel better after that."

"Nooo," she wailed.

I sighed. The reassurance gambit wasn't working. Maybe if I just heard her out, she would realize how ridiculous her suspicion was. "Okay, tell me about it," I said.

"Not on the phone. They could be listening in. I've already said too much. You have to come over."

I rolled my eyes. "Let me get back to you shortly," I said, and hung up.

The devil on my left shoulder told me to blow her off; the angel on my right urged me to go. I needed a tie-breaker. I looked around the swamp for my companion, Lana. She's six feet of muscle and mouth. Her skin is habitually cracked and mud-caked. Her eyeballs bulge, and one snaggletooth juts out over her upper lip.

No, she's not a butch women's basketball coach or a Catholic school nun. She's an American alligator.

I spotted her ridged back emerging from the mire. I informed her of my dilemma. She rolled onto her back, exposing her ghastly white underbelly to the warmth of the sun.

Hello? I said in my mind. *Are you listening? I need input here.*

She swished her tail, maneuvering herself out of the shadow of an overhanging cypress branch into a sunnier spot.

Bullshit, seemed to be the message. *You already know the right thing to do. You always do. You just go through this charade of consulting me, hoping I'll tell you what you want to hear and absolve you of responsibility. As a matter of fact, I've been meaning to discuss this with you. I'm starting to feel used.*

Look, I said, *can we have this "where is this relationship going" chat later? Just tell me what it is you think I know, already. Should I stay or should I go?*

She flipped back over and went out into the vast unknown of the River of Grass. I guess that was her signal for me to go, too. *Damn.*

I dialed the number Gitta had called from. She answered before the first ring was complete. "Harriet, thank God."

"When's a good time for me to come by?" I asked.

"This instant!" she hissed. That was the addictive mindset for you—the need for immediate gratification with no regard for other people.

"I'll be there in a couple hours," I said. In fact, the journey wouldn't take more than an hour, but I didn't want her to think I was at her beck and call.

Now, you might wonder why Gitta was seeking my help in the first place. After all, Reilly was a homicide cop—why not go to him? Well, for all I knew, she might have gone to him, too. But this was not my first ride at the murder rodeo. I'm a private investigator, although my specialty is scams, not skeletons. I run a one-woman operation, Scam-Busters. The Great Recession has had no negative impact on my business; South Florida is still Scam Central USA. The nature of the crime has simply shifted from deceptive derivatives and ninja (no income, no job or assets) loans to foreclosure fraud and bogus bankruptcy bailouts.

Despite my clear specialization, people keep coming to me with killings. I guess it's like being a doctor. You might be a pediatric podiatrist, but that doesn't stop people from asking your advice on their pathological prostates. They hear the "doctor" part but not the "specialist" part. So it is for the poor PI.

But why do I take these cases, you might ask? Is it an inability to just say no? In a word, yes. You see, it's something deep inside me—my Inner Vigilante. Whenever I get a whiff of injustice, I have to set it right. And I've learned that doing so often requires action beyond the law, just as Dirty Harry, that rogue cop of '70s movie fame, knew. Hence my moniker, "Dirty Harriet," bestowed on me by the media following that little business of my husband's demise.

Not that I believed the matter at hand was really murder, as I said. I'd ride out to The Oasis, placate Gitta's paranoia, and be back home in time to enjoy the sunset over the swamp, my habitual glass of Hennessy in hand.

I finished polishing the spokes of my Hog and maneuvered the bike onto the customized airboat moored to the hitching post at the side of my porch. The vessel is a former tourist boat originally designed to carry a dozen people, retrofitted to accommodate me and my Hog, tied down with straps (just the Hog, not me).

I cast off the ropes, inserted plugs into my ears, topped them with noise-cancelling headphones, and turned on the engine. When it comes to motors, there's only one sound that speaks to me—the one-of-a-kind, offbeat rhythm of the Harley Davidson V-twin. Whereas a Hog is the roar of a wild tiger, the motor that spins the five-foot fan on the back of an airboat is the screech of ten thousand housecats in heat. Hence the ear protection.

When I engaged the gears, the boat glided away from my stilt-elevated log cabin. I looked back fondly at my home, a little . . . well, oasis in the watery wilderness. I've equipped the place with a generator and self-composting septic tank. Hauling in gas, water, and food once a week allows me complete self-sufficiency.

As I skimmed over the surface of the shallow water, the sawgrass parted before me, and flocks of snowy egrets took flight. The sky was big and round out here. I'd once lived in a huge house with a small slice of sky; now I lived in a small house with a huge hunk of heaven. My freedom was inversely proportional to the size of my dwelling.

As I breathed in the smells of nature—the lake water, the pine trees, and, okay, exhaust fumes—I felt my phone vibrate in my hip pocket. Damn, was Gitta calling again? What was it now? She couldn't get a massage on demand? Had the manicurists gone on strike?

I looked at the display. It wasn't Gitta. It was Lior. My . . . Krav Maga martial arts instructor. Except he was more than that now. Something had been building between us over the past six months, and it had culminated in a near-consummation of our relationship during the height of the hurricane two months ago. However, homicidal interests had intervened.

Immediately thereafter, Lior had flown to his native Israel for what was supposed to be a quick wrap-up of some unfinished business. However, his stay had been extended for reasons unknown to me. Reasons that would probably remain unknown, since, as Lior had disclosed to me, he wasn't merely a personal trainer. That was just a cover for his real job—Interpol agent. Just when we had gotten closer, secrets had surfaced. Secrets that might bind us—or unravel us.

I turned off the boat's motor, removed my headgear, and answered the phone. "Hey." I wasn't the warm-and-fuzzy-greeting type.

"Hi, baby." His Hebrew-accented baritone sent electricity from my head to my . . . uh, toes. "Miss me?" he asked. The man had a certain arrogance. Not enough to qualify for asshole status but annoying nonetheless.

Yeah, I missed his six-foot-four, rock-solid self. "Nope," I said.

"You know me—loner to the core. Lana's all the company I need."

"That's too bad, seeing as I'll be home tomorrow evening. I guess you won't be glad to see me." I could just feel him smirk from across the Atlantic.

I froze. Tomorrow? Well, it wasn't like I had to rush to get my hair done, my legs waxed, and buy expensive-but-trashy lingerie. Those days were behind me. Okay, so I still favored lacy thongs and matching push-up bras—although as I approached forty (on Wednesday—three days away!), the latter were becoming a necessity rather than a luxury.

As far as the rest, I shaved every day, and I had a hair routine— pulling my long, dark wavy locks into a ponytail. Took all of three seconds. So I was not about to make myself over for a man. I'd already travelled the road from artifice to authenticity that Gitta was now embarking on. Which made me, I guess, kind of a mentor to her.

But still, the thought of seeing Lior again following our interrupted intimate encounter and his abrupt departure gave me pause. In truth, the past two months had allowed me to put off thinking about our relationship. Now it was in my face.

An osprey glided overhead, settling into a large nest atop a gumbo limbo tree.

"You arrive tomorrow?" I said. "Cool. Need a ride from the airport?"

"Sure. Straddling behind you with your hair in my face will be just what I need after a twelve-hour flight."

For a moment I didn't know whether he was being sincere or sarcastic. But Lior wasn't the sarcastic type. That would be me.

He gave me the flight details. Then his voice got softer. "See you soon." And he was gone.

Gazing at my navigational monitor, I saw that the boat had drifted off course while I'd been preoccupied. I replaced my hearing protection, restarted the engine, and turned back toward the dock that was my destination. It was located on the far western edge of Boca, where the land ended and the no-man's-land began.

The transition from wilderness to civilization was abrupt. One moment I was surrounded by nothing but sawgrass and swamp, the next moment I broke through to the wooden pier and asphalt road beyond. I pulled beside the dock, tied up the vessel, and offloaded the Hog.

I donned my helmet and leathers. I might be a thrill-seeker, but I'm not foolhardy. Riding without protection was a death wish. If that's what I'd wanted, I would have just stayed with Bruce.

The 883-cc Sportster was just the right size for my five-foot-six frame. My boots rested solidly on the earth, and my gloved hands gripped the handlebars at just below shoulder height. It was all ergonomically correct. I pulled in the clutch with my left hand, pushed the starter button with my right, and the tiger awoke.

I shifted into first by pushing down the lever with my left toe, slowly let out the clutch, and twisted the throttle with my right hand. Let me tell you, riding a Hog means being intimately involved with the machine—no autopilot on these babies.

I took off down the straight two-lane bordered on both sides with canals and the occasional palm tree. There was no traffic out here, so I was able to cruise at a good clip. In motorcycle moments like this, it can feel like you're standing still while the world whizzes past you. It's an Einsteinian relativity thing.

However, that sensation stops when you hit the outskirts of town, and cars—or cages, as we bikers call them—crop up. Then you've got to be hyper vigilant for all the clueless kooks out there who could kill you.

So I slowed down as the Mediterranean-style McMansions of the Boca 'burbs came into view. I crossed Highway 441, where my office was located, and buzzed eastward, toward the Atlantic. Now the road was lined with perfectly manicured grass and hedges surrounding swanky subdivisions.

The Oasis was located in a former luxury condo complex that had been under construction when the housing bubble burst. Financing had evaporated, and the unfinished structure, with its rebar sticking up out of grey concrete block and its dirt lot overrun with rats, had been a blight on Boca for years. About a year ago, an out-of-town corporation bought the property and repurposed it as a drying-out hideaway for the likes of Lindsay Lohan. The client list was, of course, top secret, but occasionally the *Inquisitor*, our very own hometown tabloid, got the scoop on an infamous inmate . . . er, patient, and splashed the "news" on the front page.

I pulled up to the guard house of the compound . . . I mean, complex. The rent-a-cop inside looked like a military reject. His blue uniform hung on his scrawny frame, and his face was in need of a good acne cream. Guys like that probably shouldn't be allowed to bear arms. He'd be no match for me and my snub-nose Magnum. The one I had license to carry concealed—and did, in my boot.

"Driver's license, please, ma'am," he said.

Now do you see my point? The kid was a danger to himself. Anyone who addresses any woman as "ma'am" puts himself in peril. It should always be "Miss," even to a centenarian. And don't call me testy just because I'll be hitting the big four-oh next week.

I was about to produce my ID when some kind of warning bell went off in my head. On the outside chance that there was any truth to Gitta's claims, maybe I should be circumspect. I handed over my alternate ID instead—the one identifying me as Hailey Holloway and listing a vacant lot as my address. The guy consulted his computer.

"I'm sorry, ma'am, you're not on the visitors list," he said.

"Oh." I thought for a second. "Well, that's because I'm not visiting anyone. I want to speak with someone about . . . uh, getting my sister into treatment."

He looked me up and down. "Your sister. Right."

I guess he'd heard that one before.

"Please go ahead to the front entrance, and someone from the intake department will meet you and hook you up," he said.

Hook me up? To what, exactly? An electroshock machine? Visions of Jack Nicholson in *One Flew Over the Cuckoo's Nest* floated through my head.

The guard logged my information and handed my card back to me. The ornate wrought iron gate swung open, allowing me entry into the asylum.

A lush green lawn spread out before me, lined with flower beds. Don't ask me what kind. I know Hogs, not horticulture.

A short, wiry man—a Haitian, I judged from his broad face and mahogany skin—stood holding a hose attached to a plastic tank atop the bed of a small truck. He was spraying the lawn with a green liquid. In Boca, lawns were always green, though not necessarily naturally.

I parked the Hog in the lot filled with Benzes and Lexuses (Lexi?). I took off my helmet, propped it on the backrest, and stashed my leather chaps and jacket in the saddlebags.

Then I looked at the fortress . . . er, facility. The building was a three-story structure designed in a Moorish style, with horseshoe arches, rounded domes, and mosaic-tiled walls. It was Arabian Nights for Addicts.

No one was in sight. Bypassing the front double doors and resisting the urge to say, "Open Sesame," I walked around the side of the building and called Gitta on my cell.

"Harriet! Where are you?" she whispered.

"Outside the building."

I heard a gush of expelled air as she breathed out. "Oh, what a relief. But wait. You can't come inside. I don't want them to know about you."

"Already got that covered. Can you come out?"

"Yes. I'll meet you out back. There's a maze there."

A maze? What the hell did that mean? But she had already hung up.

I walked along the side of the building, passing a large, three-tiered fountain, its water splashing melodically. Around it, a half-dozen middle-aged men led by a younger one, all clad in loose attire, moved their limbs in slow motion. T'ai Chi. They call that a martial art? Their snail's pace made me want to spring some Krav Maga action on them. Show them what real combat is all about.

Behind the building, another vast lawn stretched to the Intracoastal Waterway, where gentle waves shimmered in the sun. Near the edge was an Olympic-size pool. A few women who should have realized their bikini days were over splashed around, led by a perky instructor doing water aerobics. They call that exercise? It's child's play. I expected them to start calling out "Marco" and "Polo" any minute.

To the side of the pool I saw a long hedge that was over six feet tall. In the middle of it was a trellised opening with a small iron gate. I walked over. A metal sign by the gate read:

Meditation Maze

Walking labyrinths have been used since ancient times to enhance serenity and spirituality. Modern science has shown that mazes evoke the relaxation response, leading to improved blood pressure, breathing rate, chronic pain, insomnia, and fertility.

Enter and Peace Be With You.

With all those promises, they should have called it the Miracle Maze.

I opened the gate and entered. In front of me was another hedge, equally tall. The two shrub walls bordered a pathway leading in both directions. I stepped aside and breathed in the scent of freshly-cut foliage. I listened to the gentle water sounds coming from the pool and fountain. Damned if I wasn't starting to relax.

Then the gate opened. A tall, slender woman with long blonde hair entered, wearing white linen palazzo pants and a matching sleeveless top. Gitta.

She looked furtively to her left and right. When she saw me she hustled over, grabbed my bare arm with one hand, and dug in her French-manicured silk-wrap nails. With her other hand, she pushed her oversize Armani sunglasses atop her head as she looked down at me.

Her pupils were dilated. Due to adrenaline, I figured. She was in fight-or-flight mode. However, her eyes, as well as her nostrils, had lost their former redness. And her complexion seemed to have more natural color. Despite whatever she thought was going on at the Oasis, it looked to me like a few days of detox had done her good.

"Come on, let's walk," she said, breathless. "Nobody can overhear us out here." She linked one arm in mine and propelled me along the gravel path, stumbling in her cork-soled platform sandals. Her Boca Babe fashion sensibilities remained intact, impractical though they were. Quite a contrast to my own daily uniform of all-black body-hugging stretch jeans and tank top.

We reached the end of the path, where the outside hedge formed a corner. We turned around the end of the inside hedge and headed in the opposite direction.

"So what's going on?" I asked.

"Two patients have died in the last week." She pulled me closer. "The staff is trying to keep it hush-hush, but everyone knows about it. Some people say the victims were suffocated, other people think they were poisoned. Whatever, something evil is going on here."

"Maybe they were natural deaths," I said. "I mean, think about it. This place might have all the trappings of a spa, but basically it's a hospital for sick people. Some deaths must be inevitable."

She looked at me, wide-eyed in horror.

"Tragic," I said. "But inevitable."

"Then why would the staff be so secretive about it?"

"Gee, Gitta, I don't know . . . uh, maybe, like, for PR purposes? How would it look if the *Inquisitor* ran a headline like 'Midnight at The Oasis: Murder and Mayhem in Ritzy Rehab?'"

"I don't understand what you're saying."

"You know, like all the major league sports teams might cancel their contracts for treating their players here. That would be a significant loss of revenue."

"Oh, yes. I see."

Of course. When anything was spelled out in dollars and cents, Boca Babes understood perfectly.

We reached a fork in the path. We could continue straight ahead or make a right turn.

"Which way do you think leads to greater peace?" I asked.

"What?"

"Never mind." I pulled her to the right. "Okay, so who are these patients who died?"

"I don't know their names, but they were a boy and a girl in the adolescent unit." Her nails dug into my arm again. "Anyone could be next. Like me!"

I stopped walking and faced her. "Gitta, I hate to break the news to you, but you are not an adolescent. Your *children* are adolescents, for God's sake." If I recalled correctly, her son, Lars, was about seventeen, and her middle one, Margitta, was a few years younger. Her youngest was a girl, but damned if I could remember her name and age. As far as I was concerned, all kids were basically indistinguishable and to be avoided until they reached the age of reason. Which would be about thirty.

Anyway, Gitta seemed to think that she hadn't aged since her beauty pageant days. Another sign that she was delusional.

"Have you talked to Reilly about this?" I asked.

"No. He'd think I was crazy."

Duh. "And I wouldn't?"

"Well, maybe you do, but that doesn't matter."

"Say what?"

She stopped and placed a hand on a hip. "I am trying to start a lasting relationship with Kevin," she said, looking at me. "How far do you think it would go if he believed I was a nutcase?"

A nutcase or a cokehead—I didn't know which Reilly would prefer. But I kept my mouth shut.

"As for you," she continued, "we've known each other over ten years. I'm not trying to start anything with you. So I don't care what you think of me."

Here's the thing about Gitta: she's often actually logical—in a very convoluted way.

She resumed walking, and I strode alongside. We reached another crossroads and veered to the left.

"If you're so scared," I said, "why don't you just leave? It's not like you're a prisoner here."

"It's Kevin, again. He'd be disappointed."

I was about to lecture her that she had to commit to sobriety for herself, not for any man. But she surprised me by beating me to the punch.

"Actually, it's more than Kevin," she said. "It's me. I want to get better. I can see that cocaine . . . well, it will kill me one day."

She had that right. It had killed Bruce. Well, *I* had killed Bruce, but only after he threatened me in a coke-induced craze. One way or another, the drugs always got you in the end.

"But you could check into another facility," I said.

"Not around here. I want to stay close to my kids. They can visit me here every day, and we can participate in the family therapy program together." She gingerly wiped a tear from an eyelash, careful not to smear her mascara. "My drug use has affected them, I can see that now. Like how they've covered for me or flushed my stash down the toilet. I should never have put them in that position."

I had to admit I admired her insight and resolve. But I didn't see how I could help. Besides, the deaths were probably natural, as I'd said.

We rounded another corner.

Gitta let out an ear-splitting scream.

On the path ahead of us a pair of white Nikes pointed to the sky. They were attached to a pair of baggy jeans. A hand rested on an empty, plastic Coke bottle.

It was a teenage boy. With a pair of hedge clippers sticking up out of his chest.

Chapter 2

"STOP SCREAMING!" I snapped at Gitta. Like that would do any good. She kept right on.

I looked away from her, back to the body. The boy was black with close-cropped hair, nearly shaved bald. His eyes were open, staring blankly at the sky. I had the urge to close his lids to give him some semblance of serenity and dignity, but of course I couldn't.

A dark stain of blood emanated from the stab wound in his chest, where the hedge clippers were embedded all the way to their handles. Whoever had plunged in that instrument had either had extreme strength or extreme adrenaline.

My stomach turned, and I had an immediate urge to flee.

But where would I go? I could be trapped in this freaking maze forever. Besides, once the cops arrived, they'd put the whole place on lockdown.

Yet, another part of me was telling me to stay. I recognized it—my Inner Vigilante. Now that Gitta's seemingly paranoid fears had turned out be grounded in reality, I had to get justice for this poor boy.

Gitta was still screaming. I heard pounding footsteps.

"Where are you?" a man's voice yelled.

"Over here!" Gitta screamed.

More voices.

"We've gone the wrong way!" a woman said.

"Well, what's the right way?" A different male voice asked.

"I don't know!" The woman again.

Moments later, the entire troupes of T'ai Chi masters and water sprites burst around the corner of the hedge, headed by the two group leaders, who were presumably staff members. When they saw the body, everyone stopped, crowding the narrow pathway.

"Oh my God, it's Demarcus Pritchett," the female staff member screamed. "From the adolescent unit."

Now he had a name—an identity. He wasn't just a body anymore.

More screams and pandemonium ensued. The men and women

quickly assumed traditional gender roles, with the alpha hero guys wrapping their arms around the dripping damsels in distress.

"Calm down, everyone," the male T'ai Chi leader said. This failed to get anyone's attention.

The female staff member was the youngest of the women, yet the only one wearing a one-piece swimsuit instead of two. She looked like she belonged in Sea World performing tricks with dolphins and whales. Instead, she was trying to separate the clinging couples. "Tyler, please let go of Skyler," she said, sounding like she was talking to preschoolers.

Tyler pulled Skyler closer.

I knew that romantic relationships among people in treatment were discouraged because they distracted people from their own recovery and fostered co-dependency. (Listen, I'd read my share of self-help books during and after my marital implosion. Or explosion, to be technically accurate). And, of course, shared traumatic crises like this were perfect breeding grounds for future doomed romances.

It was clear that someone needed to take charge of the scene. And it was equally clear that it would have to be me.

"Everyone stand back," I said. "This is a crime scene. We must not contaminate the evidence."

To my own amazement, my pronouncement worked. Maybe it was my authoritative voice or my menacing biker bearing. Or maybe it was that everyone was so brainwashed by watching *CSI* and *NCIS* and god knows how many other forensic crime shows on TV, that like docile sheep, they accepted my command. Even Gitta wound down.

But now I had a major dilemma. I'd entered the premises under false pretenses. How would I explain that to the cops? And if I called the cops on my cell, they'd know my real identity immediately. I assumed the patients' phones were confiscated upon check-in, since Gitta had called me from a landline in the facility. That left the two staff people.

The woman was trying to pry the prickly pairs apart. I turned to the man, who was now pacing back and forth, taking deep breaths. He was a sandy-haired surfer type, dressed in board shorts and a t-shirt.

"What's your name?" I asked.

"Sandy," he said.

Sometimes life totally lacked irony. It was disconcerting, a bizarre twist in the universe that I had not yet come to wrap my mind around.

"Sandy, will you please call 911," I said.

"Uh, sure, dude." He pulled out his cell phone and punched the numbers. Then he reported the details in a perfectly professional manner, thus restoring order to my ironic world.

"I'd better call the CEO and Medical Director, too," he said, demonstrating a keen grasp of the organizational culture. Namely, his bosses would have his ass if he left them out of the loop. He stabbed at his screen some more as the sun beat down overhead.

Figuring we had a couple minutes before the officers and the officials arrived, I took the time to more closely examine the body and the scene.

The boy's Nikes were scuffed, and the bottoms of his jeans were frayed. He wore a checked, short-sleeved button-down shirt that was a far cry from American Eagle or whatever else was the height of current teen fashion. All in all, he was not the picture of affluence that befit Boca in general and The Oasis in particular.

While the boy's left hand was splayed on the empty Coke bottle, his right hand clutched some torn sheets of paper. They looked like newsprint. I bent and peered closer. They weren't a newspaper—they were pages from a phone book. The Yellow Pages. The R's, though I couldn't make out more detail than that.

Where was the rest of the book? Had he torn these pages out and left the book elsewhere—or had he and the killer fought over it?

The grass around the body was trampled, and the hedges were crushed as though someone had fallen into them. Apparently, there had been a struggle. The kid hadn't just been laying there sunbathing when someone came along and stabbed him.

I heard rustling in the hedges.

"Dammit, with all these crises, I may have to cancel my annual vacation to Italy," a woman's husky voice said.

"That's the least of our problems right now, Maria," a man replied, panting for breath.

The two came around the corner of the tall, dense foliage. The man appeared to be in his forties. So did his body mass index. Rivulets of sweat poured down his face, and his white shirt was drenched. He was hardly the image of health that you'd think The Oasis would want to project. Irony was intact. But I feared we'd have another dead body any minute.

The woman appeared to be younger, although you never could tell in Boca. She wore a butter-yellow suit that matched her shoulder-length hair, topped by a white doctor's coat with "Maria Stillwater, MD" stitched on the pocket. Maybe she could save her companion in the event of a heart attack.

"Dr. Stillwater! Mr. Evans! Thank God you're here," Sandy said. As if they had the power to make this tragedy disappear. Then again, this was Boca—maybe they did.

The doctor knelt by the body, removed a stethoscope from around her neck, placed it in her ears and listened to the boy's chest. As if it weren't obvious that he was dead. But I guess she had to do what she was trained to. She shook her head as she removed the earpiece and replaced the instrument. "Poor Demarcus," she murmured.

She stood and looked at the two staff members. "What happened?" she asked.

"When we got here," Miss Sea World spoke up, "these two were here with . . ." she trailed off as she pointed to me, Gitta, and the body.

"Mrs. Castellano," the doctor nodded to Gitta. "And who are you?" she asked me.

"Hailey Holloway," I said. Gitta shot me a look, eyebrows raised (as far as they would go on her Botoxed forehead, that is). I shot her a discreet kick to the ankle to keep her quiet about my name change. Evidently she got the message, as she kept her lips sealed.

"You're not a patient," Dr. Stillwater said. "I see all our patients on admission. Are you a visitor?"

"Uh, I came to speak with someone about getting help for my sister."

"Oh please, Ms. Holloway, that's the oldest line in the book. I've been in this business a long time. Don't try that one on me, honey. It's you who needs help, am I right?"

If that's what she wanted to assume, I'd go along with it. "Yes, you're right, doctor."

"Well, we can help you."

A sales pitch at a place of slaying. Only in Boca.

"But not right now, obviously," she amended, apparently sensing my distaste.

A scream of sirens sounded in the distance. It grew louder and louder, then stopped. Footsteps pounded again. The cops. Would they be ones I knew—like Reilly—who would blow my cover?

A few moments later, two male uniformed officers and a tall, brunette woman in a grey pinstriped pantsuit with a badge clipped to her belt ran around the hedge, all panting. Either they were in sad shape for cops, or, like everyone else, they'd made a few wrong turns trying to find us in the maze.

I let out a breath of relief. I didn't know any of them. I could maintain my ruse, at least for a while.

Gitta stumbled over to the plainclothes cop and grabbed her arm. That seemed to be her habit. "Janice! Where's Kevin? I thought he would come. I need him,"

No! I thought. *Not Reilly!*

Apparently the two women were acquainted. Janice patted Gitta's hand. "Mrs. Castellano, Detective Reilly can't be involved in this case because his personal relationship with you would create conflict of interest. I'll be the primary investigator here. Detective Reilly can visit you but not in an official capacity. Now please, let me do my work." She pried Gitta's fingers off her arm.

"Everyone," she announced to the group, "I'm Detective Snyder, Boca Raton PD. I need you all to please go inside the building. These officers will interview each of you. No one leaves the grounds until our crime scene investigation is complete and witness statements are taken. We have officers stationed at the exit. And we have a patrol boat on the Intracoastal side, so no one can leave that way, either. We appreciate your cooperation."

That was a nice way of saying we were all prisoners.

Gitta took hold of my hand as the uniformed officers ushered everyone out of the maze. Or tried to. No one seemed to know where they were going. We kept turning corners only to find ourselves boxed in by more hedges. The patients were starting to panic, and I lost my patience.

"Hold on, everybody," I said. I took out my cell and accessed an aerial view of the maze from Google Earth. "Follow me."

The cops glared at me then at each other. "Follow her," one of them said with a sigh. "We'll bring up the rear."

Phone in hand, I led the way out. I'd never felt so much like a rat in all my life.

Once we were on the open lawn, the officers reclaimed their control and herded us to the building. When I stepped over the threshold of that Moorish entryway, a feeling that had been nagging at the corners of my mind ever since I'd bluffed my way onto the grounds now hit me with full force. It was my Inner Vigilante, telling me I had to get justice for that poor dead boy. I couldn't just turn my back on this vicious act and walk away. The police would pursue the official lines of inquiry. But an insider might discover something they couldn't.

I had to check myself—er, Hailey Holloway—into The Oasis.

Chapter 3

"EVERYONE, PLEASE take a seat here in the lobby," one of the uniforms said.

I took a look around. The Kasbah theme continued on the interior of the building, with marble tiled floors, patterned mosaic walls, and recessed seating niches plumped with rich jewel-toned pillows. No hookah pipes were in sight, though. Guess that might be just a tad inappropriate. However, I half-expected some belly dancers to come prancing out any minute.

A receptionist came around a gleaming pink granite counter. Rather than harem pants and a bare midriff, she wore standard-issue Boca Babe wannabe attire: miniskirt and sheer top revealing a lace bra. The wannabes were the ones who had not yet mastered the distinction between sexy and skanky.

"What's going on?" she asked no one in particular.

Before anyone could reply, Stillwater and Evans rushed through the door. (Hey, they sound like an old-school rock band, don't they?) They hurried to the receptionist and started talking in hushed tones. I could just make out the words *media, damage control,* and *corporate crisis consultant.* The wheels of the spin machine were being set in motion.

"Folks," one of the cops said, "I'm Officer Hernandez. This is Officer Fernandez."

How was I supposed to keep them apart in my mind? I looked them up and down, searching for visual cues that I could pair with their names. A little mnemonic trick I learned while in PI training with Louie, my mentor.

Both were young, in their early twenties. Same height—tall; same bearing—upright. And both had a look of suppressed excitement in their eyes that told me they were rookies working their first homicide. Okay—Hernandez had hair; Fernandez, though bald, had facial fuzz. H's and F's. Got it.

"As Detective Snyder stated," Hernandez continued, "we'll interview each of you. First, we need to take down all your names."

After they did that, Hernandez said, "Now, we need everyone to wait their turn alone." He turned to the conferring trio of staff members. "Are there holding cells . . . I mean, rooms, where we could place the suspects . . . I mean, witnesses?"

Stillwater stepped forward. "Yes, of course. The clients can wait in their rooms. We have private accommodations only. No roommates. Please, everyone, go ahead to your quarters and stay there until you're called."

"And no talking or calling each other," Hernandez said.

That was his first rookie mistake. Never trust a suspect—I mean, witness—to do as you say.

The patients rose and walked off.

Gitta grabbed my hands, crushing my fingers as she mouthed "Don't leave me!"

I pulled out of her grasp and patted her arm. "I won't," I whispered.

After the departures, I was left in the lobby with Miss Sea World and Surfer Sandy.

"Where can we interview the witnesses?" Fernandez asked Hall & Oates. I mean, Stillwater & Evans.

"You may use our offices," Stillwater said. Evans may have been the titular CEO of this operation, but it looked like Stillwater held the reins.

"Tifanni, you'll show the officers the way," she commanded the receptionist.

"Certainly, doctor."

"So, who was first on the scene?" Hernandez asked.

I raised my hand.

"Follow me. Fernandez, you take her." He gestured to Miss Sea World. Then he turned to Sandy. "You wait here, please."

I followed Hernandez, who followed Tifanni, down a short hallway. The walls were lined with the black-framed motivational posters you see in those catalogs stuffed into the backs of airplane seats: photos of eagles, mountains, and rainbows with messages like *Aim High! Believe and Succeed! Dare to Soar!* Gag me!

Tifanni unlocked a door, stood aside to let us in, and left, closing the door behind her. The room had a large window looking out onto a courtyard filled with lush tropical plants and was furnished with the usual markers of corporate status: heavy, dark wood desk, high-backed leather and brass-studded chairs, sofa, coffee table, bookcases, and walls lined with diplomas, commendations, and photos of Stillwater posing with local muckety-mucks. I noticed my old friend, the Contessa von Phul, bigwig Boca philanthropist, among them. Hmm. Her connection could come in handy.

Hernandez took the throne behind the desk and gestured for me to take one of the smaller chairs in front. Guess he'd learned all about Using Space for Power in Police Academy 101.

The sunlight beaming through the glass behind him gave a glow to his jet-black hair. His shirt buttons and the badge on his chest pocket gleamed, and the radio clipped to his epaulet gave him an air of authority. I had to admit, there was something compelling about a man in uniform. The feeling disturbed me. After all, I was a vigilante warrior woman. I wasn't supposed to fall prey to such sexist fairy tale fantasies.

He whipped out a tablet and started tapping the screen. "May I see some ID, please," he said.

I hesitated before handing over the fake card. If I was found out, I could be charged with fraud and obstruction of justice. I'd lose my PI license. But then, I knew all about the criminal justice system—especially the Boca variety. It did not always serve the victims—particularly if they were poor, as Demarcus appeared to be. My Inner Vigilante won out, and I passed Hailey Holloway's driver's license to Hernandez.

After he logged in the info he said, "So tell me exactly how you arrived on the scene, what you saw and heard."

I recounted everything from my entry onto the grounds to the point when he himself arrived. Of course, my story was judiciously edited and embellished. Not the facts surrounding the discovery of the boy. Just my reason for being there.

As I talked, he tapped.

"So, you say you're a friend of Mrs. Brigitta Larsen O'Malley Castellano, a patient here, who has encouraged you to check yourself in?"

"Yes."

"But you told the security guard and Dr. Stillwater that you were here about your sister."

"Well, yes . . . you know how it is . . . I wasn't ready to admit I needed help."

"And now you are?"

"Um, not really. Especially now with this killing of that poor child. What if the other patients are in danger?"

"I have no way of knowing at this point whether this is an isolated incident. But I can assure you Detective Snyder will investigate to the fullest extent of the law. Whether you want to stay here or not, that's up to you. We have your contact info, so we know how to reach you if we need to."

Right. The shit would hit the fan once the cops found out Hailey Holloway lived in a vacant lot in one of the abandoned developments that had come to dot Boca over the last few years.

"So I'm free to go?" I asked.

"Yes, I'll walk back out to reception with you."

Guess he didn't trust me not to make any unsanctioned detours on the way. And rightly so. I'd planned to peer into some offices and snoop through file cabinets and wastebaskets. Such fun would have to wait.

We made our way back to Tifanni. Hernandez asked her to hail Gitta and bring her to the interrogation room, then he headed back there.

Shit! Gitta! We had to get our stories straight before she talked to Hernandez.

I went into a coughing fit.

"Are you all right?" Tifanni asked.

"No," I gasped. "I think my asthma is acting up." I wheezed. "Could you please bring me a glass of water?" Like that would help constricting lungs. But I was betting she didn't know that. And I was right.

"Of course," she said. "Do you prefer Evian, Perrier, or San Pellegrino?"

Jesus. "Just"—gasp—"tap water."

She took off for a back room.

I whipped out my phone and pushed "redial."

Gitta picked up immediately. "Harriet? I—"

"Listen very carefully," I cut her off. "My name is Hailey Holloway. We're old friends. I have an alcohol problem. You encouraged me to check myself in here. That is exactly what you're telling the police officer."

"But—"

"Do what I say, or I'll end up in jail!" I said and hung up just as Tifanni came out with a glass of water, complete with lemon slice resting on the rim.

"Thank you," I rasped and gulped it down. "I'm okay now. Thank you so much. Um, I'll just go sit down for a while."

"Certainly."

I made my way to one of the seating niches in the lobby, where I stayed out of sight as Tifanni phoned Gitta. A couple minutes later, I heard the tapping of heels. Peering around a potted palm, I saw Gitta arrive. Tiffani led her toward the interview room. When Tiffani returned and settled in, I approached her counter again.

"Oh," she said when she looked up from her phone, on which she was either texting, gaming, or doing anything else besides actually working. "I thought you'd left." She frowned.

"No. Um, I'd like to check myself in."

"I see." Now she flashed me a bright smile. Ever since the cost of laser teeth whitening had plunged from $699 at Boca dental offices to $39.99 at the Festival Flea Market in neighboring Pompano Beach, everyone in Boca, even the Babe wannabes, had blinding choppers. And of course, everyone had a smile ready when cash was about to be forked over.

"Stay right here," Tifanni said, clearly not one to let a live one get away. "I'll call one of our intake counselors, and they'll be with you right away."

True to Tiffani's word, seconds later, a thirtyish, sporty woman with short brown hair, flashing yet another laser smile, approached, hand outstretched. "Hi, I'm Paula."

I didn't respond immediately, feigning the delayed reaction time I'd observed among various substance abusers of my acquaintance.

"And you are?" she asked.

"Oh. Hailey," I said, taking her hand. She had a firm grip, perhaps from wielding a tennis racket, if her biceps and lateral delts, displayed by her sleeveless pink top, were any indication.

"It's very nice to meet you, Hailey."

Spoken like a true sales pro. Always tack your mark's name onto your utterances. It's exactly how scam artists operate, too. Gives people a false sense of intimacy.

"Why don't we go to my office and chat," Paula said. "Can I get you anything to drink?"

"A mojito?"

She wasn't fazed. "How about an herbal horehound tea?"

Whorehound? I didn't even want to go there. "Uh, no thanks."

If that's the kind of thing the patients drank here, what the hell did they eat? Sautéed seaweed? Toasted tofu? Braised blood sausage? I might not last long without my ritual nightcap of Hennessy and my daily diet of hamburgers, ravioli, salami sticks . . . On the other hand, my big four-oh was looming. Maybe an enforced frou-frou organic regimen would drop-kick me into healthier habits.

I followed Paula back down the same hallway I'd just left into an office a few doors down from Dr. Stillwater's. The room was smaller than the top dog's, and there was no picturesque window. A nameplate on the desk had more initials following Paula's name than there were letters in it: Paula Green, BA, MSW, LCSW, BCD, ACSW, LMFT, CAC. Damn, she almost had the entire alphabet covered. At this rate, she'd soon run out of characters and have to resort to Greek or Hebrew.

People who had to advertise their status that way always made me wary. It bespoke either a lack of confidence, an abundance of arrogance, or yet again, a scam. Hey, what can I say? Seeing scams everywhere is an occupational hazard for a Scam Buster. Kind of like seeing assholes everywhere is an occupational hazard for a proctologist.

A couple easy chairs were crammed into the corner of the room. Paula gestured to one and took the other.

"So, Hailey, tell me what brings you here today," she said as I sat.

I wrung my hands as I looked down at my lap.

"It wasn't my idea. But my friend Gitta—she's a patient here—she's been ragging on me to check myself in."

"I see. And why do you think she's been doing that?"

"I'll tell you why. Now that she's been clean and sober for what— like, a whole two weeks?—it's like she's drunk the Kool Aid, and now she wants to convert everyone to her newfound lifestyle. I'm happy for her, but that doesn't mean it's for everyone. That girl was a cokehead. I don't do drugs. You know what? I don't need this crap. I'm gonna go." I rose and headed for the door. An inspired bit of theatrics, if I do say so myself.

"Hold on, Hailey." Paula put a manicured hand on my arm. "You're free to go, of course, but since you're already here, we might as well talk a little more so that you haven't totally wasted your time. What do you say?"

I rolled my eyes. "I guess." I sat back down.

"Well, *I* guess," Paula said, "that some little part of you, deep inside, is thinking that, just maybe, you might have an addiction problem. Something in what your friend said has hit home. Otherwise, you wouldn't be here at all."

I shrugged.

"You said you don't do drugs—so why do you think your friend suggested you come here?"

"She says I have an alcohol problem. But that's bullshit."

"You do realize alcohol is a drug, right?"

"No! I'm not a druggie like Gitta and everybody else here. I drink because I like to, not because I have to. I can quit any time I want."

"Have you ever tried to quit?"

"No. I don't want to."

"Okay. How about if I read you a few questions from a brief screening test? This will give us an indication of whether alcohol might be a problem for you."

"Sure. That's a good idea. Because I can tell you it's not."

She leaned over to a file cabinet, pulled out a sheet of paper, and attached it to a clipboard. She ran through about a dozen questions about the frequency and quantity of my drinking, whether I was always able to stop once I started, whether I'd ever blacked out, and so on. I made it up as we went along.

"Well, Hailey, according to your score, alcohol may indeed be causing some difficulties in your life."

Right. I bet that was the standard line they used on everybody.

"The good news is, you're not alone. We're here to help. This is something you can overcome."

Yeah. At a price.

"How much does it cost to get treated here?" I asked.

"We offer a 28 day inpatient program that is completely comprehensive."

Completely comprehensive. Is there anything that's comprehensive but not complete? Or complete but not comprehensive?

People say I'm a woman of few words, just like Dirty Harry (except that he was a man). But I beg to differ. It's not that Harry and I speak few words—we speak just the right number. No more than necessary. No redundancies like "completely comprehensive." We're efficient.

"We provide a range of medical, psychiatric, psychological, social, and spiritual interventions," Paula recited. "Each treatment plan is completely individualized to each patient's needs."

There she went again. As opposed to what—partially individualized? To somebody else's needs?

"And we provide only the latest, cutting-edge, evidence-based approaches. We are partnered with the University of—"

"Yeah," I said, cutting her off. "So how much did you say it costs?"

"The inpatient program is $25,000. Then there's aftercare, which is—" This time she cut herself off. She must have heard the sound of my jaw hitting the marble floor. "Do you have insurance?" she asked.

"Yup," I said, thinking of the gun stashed in my boot. "I'm insured by Magnum Force."

She frowned. "I don't think we take that plan. If cost is a concern for you, I can refer you to the county-run program. Of course, they don't offer quite the same level of service."

No doubt. "That's okay. Actually, Gitta will cover my expenses."

I hadn't told Gitta that, but I was sure she wouldn't object. Especially seeing as how she wanted me there to save her life. Besides, I sure as hell wasn't going to be in there the whole twenty-eight . . . twenty-eight days! No way! Lior was arriving the following evening. We'd been forced apart for two months. And there was a definite, unspoken understanding about our upcoming reunion. We intended to finish what we started—our interrupted intimate encounter. Our first.

That did it. I wasn't about to be trapped in this world of the weird and the wacky when I should be doing the wild thing with my man. I had just over twenty-four hours to catch a killer.

Chapter 4

"LET ME JUST have our billing department verify your payer source," Paula said. She made a phone call and relayed what I'd told her about Gitta covering my stay. "Yes, I'll hold," she said.

A minute later she said, "Wonderful, thank you."

She hung up and turned to me. "Okay, then! Mrs. Castellano has agreed to pay for your treatment." She flashed me a shark smile that said *I'm about to get my hefty commission.* What she actually said was, "Let's get you checked in."

I half-expected her to say, "Do you prefer a king bed or a double? Smoking or non? We have free Wi-Fi, and the ice machine is just down the hall."

Instead, she said, "For the next forty-eight hours, you'll be in our Total Purification Detoxification unit, where you'll have a thorough workup done by our medical director, our psychologist, our psychiatrist, and our chaplain."

Perfect. As these gurus were poking and prodding my body, mind, and soul, I'd be doing the same to them (well, except the body part). After all, any of them could be the killer—or at least, hold a clue to the killer's identity.

"The team will develop your personalized treatment plan, and then you'll be transferred to our Whole Wonderful Woman unit," Paula said.

If you ask me, they needed to fire their branding consultant. Total Purification Detoxification put me in mind of a colonic, while Whole Wonderful Woman sounded like those educational kits we received in sixth grade from Kotex and Tampax.

Paula went to her desk, where she turned on a computer. As she logged in, I closely watched her fingers on the keyboard. She tapped out "green," which I figured was her username, followed by "bobcats98." Her password—probably her high school team mascot and year of graduation.

I created a mental image of two green bobcats, each with a huge rhinestone "98" swinging from a fat gold chain around its neck. When I needed to remember that username and password, the image and its associations would pop right up.

Paula asked a few basic questions about me—or rather, about Hailey—and entered the data into the electronic medical record. "Who would you like to put as your emergency contact?" she asked.

Oh, shit. I hadn't anticipated that.

Over the last few years, I'd gone from being a total loner to having a small core of friends. I knew I could count on any of them with my life. But which of them could be the most duplicitous? Who wouldn't hesitate a moment if asked about "Hailey?" Who could maintain my ruse, yet blow my cover if necessary?

"Leonard Goldblatt." My mother's paramour. Retired CIA operative. Perhaps my soon-to-be stepfather No. 5.

I looked up his contact info in my cell phone and recited it to Paula.

"About your cell phone," she said. "We'll take it and keep it in a secure place."

"No!" I said in mock terror. "I can't live without my phone."

"I understand. Just as you can't live without alcohol. Mobile technology has created another form of addiction. People are constantly jonesing for that next hit, whether it's a text, a tweet, or an Angry Bird killing a pig. These experiences light up the brain's reward pathways just like alcohol and other drugs. If you are to truly get clean, it all has to go."

"You've got to be kidding me," I said.

"I'm afraid not. Now is there anyone you'd like to call first, to let them know you're here?"

I got one phone call? Whoopee. Guess I'd be strip-searched next. Actually, that wasn't so far-fetched. No doubt patients tried to smuggle their stashes in here. But surely The Oasis wouldn't subject its high-end clientele to such humiliation. The rich just wouldn't stand for it. Or bend over, to be accurate.

"Yes, I will make a call," I said.

I expected her to leave to give me some privacy, but she didn't budge. I was starting to realize that the staff here was wily. Not a lot of bullshit got past them. Except my fake identity, of course. They weren't as wily as I was. Nonetheless, cracking this case would be a challenge. If the staff were behind these deaths, they had no doubt put up layers of smokescreens and firewalls to protect themselves.

Leonard's name was still up on my screen, and I tapped it to dial him.

"Hey, Harriet," he answered.

"Hi Leonard, it's Hailey Holloway."

There was the briefest of pauses. "Yes, Hailey. What do you need me to do?"

"Listen, you know, uh, my friend Gitta, she went into treatment at The Oasis a couple weeks ago?"

"The Oasis. Got it."

"Well, uh, I'm finally taking her advice and checking myself in here, too."

"You're going undercover. Gitta's hired you to investigate something over there."

"Right. I'm so glad you understand."

"I'll activate the field network."

Huh? What the hell was he talking about? It sounded like something out of *Star Trek. Activate the electromagnetic shield, Mister Spock.*

He must have picked up on my confusion. "Our assets on the ground," he said.

Oh shit. He intended to mobilize the team that had assisted me on my last case. That would be my mother, the Contessa von Phul, and my best buds, Chuck—my redneck motorcycle mechanic—and his husband, Enrique—the suave security chief of the Boca Beach Hilton. I did not need this ragtag band hounding me on this one.

"That's okay," I started to say, but he went right on.

"I'll have an E & E plan in place by 1600 today."

"Pardon me?"

"Escape and evasion."

I sighed. There was no stopping this man. "Okay, Leonard. They're taking my phone now, so you won't be able to reach me this way." I was about to tell him visitors were allowed, but thought better of it.

"Not a problem. Agent Goldfinger over and out." He hung up on me.

Paula held out her hand, and I handed over my phone. She placed it in a baggie, tagged it, and gave me a receipt. She stood. "Let's go get you settled in detox, and I'll put this in our safe deposit box."

As we stepped outside the door, we were almost knocked over by a large woman of ample proportions who rushed down the hall. Her lavender polyester suit must have been stifling in the heat outside, because her dark complexion glistened from perspiration. Her grey-streaked black hair was unraveling from a carefully-smoothed bun and frizzing around her face. But it wasn't just beads of sweat rolling down her cheeks. Behind her rectangular-framed filigreed glasses, her eyes floated in pools of tears.

She barged past us and banged on the medical director's door. "Dr. Stillwater! Open up! Come out here! My boy—my poor boy!"

The door opened, and Hernandez stood there. "How may I help you, ma'am?"

"I want to know what happened to my boy!"

"And you are?"

"Gardenia LaFleur. I sent my boy here for help, and they killed him. They killed him!"

She leaned against the wall and collapsed to the floor. "My children," she sobbed. "My children."

This must have been the dead boy's mother. But what did she mean by *my children?*

Chapter 5

OFFICER HERNANDEZ knelt down next to Gardenia LaFleur, who sat on the floor, her back against the wall, head in her hands.

"Ma'am, let's get you up and into the office," he said. "I'll call for Dr. Stillwater."

He took one of her arms. Paula Green rushed over and took the other. Together they raised the distraught woman and walked her into Stillwater's office. I stood by like the passive patient I was supposed to be rather than the active agent I am.

Paula reemerged, closing the door behind her. "I'm sorry about that," she said.

"Wow, she kind of freaked me out," I said. "What did she mean about her children?"

"She's clearly distraught over this horrible . . . um, event. Just as I'm sure you are, since you found the . . . uh, body. But I can't discuss our clients. Confidentiality is paramount here at The Oasis. I'm sure you understand. You wouldn't want us to talk about you with other patients, right?"

"Right." Not unless I wanted to feed misinformation to someone, that is.

"So let's go ahead to the Total Purification unit." She led me to a door at the end of the corridor. She passed a magnetic key card through the reader on the door handle, and a small green light came on. She pushed down on the handle and opened the door. I followed her across the threshold and into the unknown.

The door clicked shut behind us with a disturbing finality. The sound caused me to flash back to the brief time I'd spent in the county jail after shooting Bruce. I repressed the shudder that passed through my body at the memory of those few days in lockup.

Looking around, I saw that the similarities between the jail and The Oasis ended at the door. Whereas the jail cell had consisted of a cot without a sheet, and a commode without a seat, this place was like the Ritz. In Morocco, I supposed. We were in a circular suite with five closed doors, each with the classic Moorish arched doorway. Instead of security cameras mounted on the walls, there were brass sconces that imparted a golden glow. The marble floor in the common area was covered in Persian rugs. Atop those sat plush velvet couches and armchairs in deep jewel tones of ruby and sapphire.

The center of the space was occupied by what had to be the world's most sumptuous nurses' station. Its circular inlaid-wood counter was befitting of the concierge desk at the aforementioned hotel. Maybe The Oasis had cashed in on some resort's going-out-of-business-everything-must-go sale.

Another Boca Babe Wannabe replica staffed the counter. She wore brown scrubs patterned with tan Louis Vuitton knock-off logos. She looked like a walking handbag. I'd seen those scrubs at the flea market. Only a wannabe would think that the House of Vuitton would stoop to designing uniforms for working women.

She stood and came around as we approached. "Hi, I'm Mercy. I'm one of the RNs here." She extended her hand.

An RN—period? No more initials than that? Wow, maybe she was an actual, normal person—as normal as they get in Boca, that is.

I shook her hand but didn't say anything, maintaining my spaced-out act.

"This is Hailey Holloway," Paula introduced me.

"Thanks, Paula," Mercy said. "I'll take it from here."

Paula gave me a squeeze on the shoulder. "Take care, Hailey. You're in good hands. You'll be just fine."

She departed the way we had entered. The only way to do so, I noted.

"Let me show you to your room," Mercy said, grabbing a clipboard.

I followed her through one of the archways into yet another lavishly furnished room. The king size bed was made up with luxury linens and coverlets, including a dozen pillows in as many shapes and sizes. What is it with this particular decorating trend? Don't you just need one pillow—two at the most? I guess they call them throw pillows because you have to throw them off the bed before you can get in.

The room also contained a sofa with yet more pillows and a small round oak table with a couple of chairs. The floor-to-ceiling window framed by brocade drapes looked out onto the front lawn. I noted that the window was one large mullioned glass pane—it didn't open. No way out through there.

I looked around the room for a security camera. None. Guess the staff had some respect for patient privacy.

There was no TV. That I wouldn't miss, since I don't have one in my log cabin, either. But there was no computer and, of course, no cell phone. There was a regular phone plugged into the wall, but I wasn't the phone-chatting type. I spent my time working, working out, riding, and, most evenings, drinking my glass of Hennessy while briefing Lana on my day. The thought of being cooped up in this room without any sources of stimulation or relaxation put me on edge.

"Um, would you happen to have any reading material?" I asked Mercy.

"You know, it's funny you should ask that. We do keep the patient rooms stocked with books and pamphlets on recovery, hope, and spirituality. Every room has always had a copy of *The Big Book of AA*. But lately, all the printed material has been disappearing. Of course, patients are free to take the materials since they are here for their benefit. But usually they don't. Until now, I mean. So I'm sorry, but we haven't yet had a chance to restock."

"So what am I supposed to do with myself in here?" I was starting to panic.

She patted my arm. "You'll be fine. It's normal to feel agitated and jittery during the detoxification phase of recovery. Those are withdrawal symptoms. It means your body is adjusting to being chemical-free. We'll be monitoring your vital signs every four hours. If you become really anxious or can't sleep, we'll give you some medication to help with that."

Say what? They got patients off drugs by giving them other drugs? Damned if they were going to shoot me up with anything.

"I don't think that will be necessary," I said.

She smiled. "We'll see. Now I'm going to take blood and urine samples."

I paused. "Why?"

"To get a general lab profile and to screen for drug metabolites."

"But I'm in good health, and like I told Paula, I use alcohol but no drugs. So these tests aren't necessary."

"Well, Hailey, nobody's forcing you into treatment. Of course you're free to go at any time. But if you want to be in our program, this is part of the protocol."

In other words, it was their way or the highway.

"Okay," I sighed.

Mercy handed me the clipboard and had me sign a consent form. Then she donned latex gloves, pulled a needle and several glass vials out of her pocket, and sucked some blood out of me. Next she produced a urine collection cup. "Let's go into the bathroom," she said.

"Um, I can manage myself. Have been since I was about two."

Mercy smiled again. It was getting annoying. "I have to observe you void."

I stared at her.

"If we don't, patients often substitute someone else's sample for their own."

"But I wasn't even planning to be here. I checked in on the spur of the moment. Why would I be carrying a urine sample with me?"

"I'm sorry, but rules are rules. We have to treat everyone the same. Now, please." She extended a hand toward the bathroom door, as if welcoming me to enter.

Oh my god. Was this investigation really worth such humiliation?

Hell, yes! Something inside me said. My Inner Vigilante. *You've got to get justice for that poor dead boy.*

I sighed. Then I remembered that I'd been through worse, once subjecting myself to a gynecological pelvic exam in order to catch a killer. I guess on the scale of personal invasiveness, peeing in front of someone wasn't that bad. And people think being a PI is glamorous.

We went into the room's private bath. Given the décor of the rest of the place, I was surprised the toilet wasn't a gold-plated throne. Just plain old porcelain. I sat down and did the deed.

When we emerged back into the bedroom, Mercy said, "Okay, now normally Dr. Stillwater would come in and do a history and physical on you, but I'm afraid she's indisposed right now."

Yeah, I'd guess so, what with a murder victim, a hysterical mother, and a killer on the loose.

"So let me find out who's available to meet with you—our psychiatrist, psychologist, or chaplain. If you'd like, you can wait on our back patio. It's very peaceful out there."

That seemed better than sitting in the sumptuous but stifling room. I followed Mercy to another of the arched doorways off the circular common area. This door, rather than leading into another room, as I had assumed, opened onto a granite-paved patio looking out onto a small pond. Lawn furniture and umbrellas were strategically scattered about. No one was out there. I wondered if I was the only patient in the detox unit.

Beyond the pond was an eight-foot concrete wall. So, no way out this way, either. Although Mercy had said I was free to leave, I started to wonder whether I—and all the other patients—were actually trapped in this place.

"Just relax, and I'll be back shortly," Mercy said.

Relax. Right. I paced around like a caged animal. Were the zookeepers watching? I looked up at the corner of the building. Yup. A security camera was mounted there. Guess they didn't want anyone drowning themselves—or someone else—in the pond.

I took some deep breaths and pondered the situation. Okay, so maybe I was trapped. Temporarily. No one could hold Dirty Harriet captive for long. In the meantime, I needed a plan of action for finding the killer. I sat on a plush, padded lounge chair to think.

Any investigation should always begin with the victim. I needed to find out about Demarcus and the other alleged dead teens. First, I needed to verify that there had in fact been other suspicious deaths, that they weren't just rumors. If there were other victims, who were they? Where were they from? Why were they there? How had they—other than Demarcus—died? Once I knew these things, I could look for patterns pointing to motives or suspects.

I could start by accessing the medical records on one of the facility's computers. There was a computer at the nurses' station in the suite, but I wouldn't have enough time to use that one. The station would always be staffed, except perhaps for brief moments when the nurse was with another patient or taking a bathroom break. I could easily be caught out in the open like that. Also, I'd have to do this at night, when fewer staff were around. My best shot at accessing a computer would mean getting through the locked door of the detox unit.

As I racked my brain trying to figure out how to do that, I saw a ripple in the pond before me. Then another.

Wait a minute. No way. It couldn't be.

But it was—a little alligator snout. I'd recognize one anywhere. But it couldn't be Lana. First of all, how the hell would she get all the way into town from the Glades? She was enterprising, but even so, I didn't think she had a mental map of all the canals, lakes, and ponds between here and there. Besides, this snout was considerably smaller than hers. This was like an adolescent alligator.

Hey! it said.

What? Did that thing just speak to me? I looked around. Guess it wasn't speaking to anyone else.

I'm Sylvester. Lana's great-nephew, it—or he, I guess—said.

Okay, I knew this conversation was all in my head. Maybe I should discuss this with the psychiatrist they were sending to evaluate me. Nah. Nope. Not happening. They'd lock me up for sure.

So you need to get through a locked door, Sylvester said.

Uh, yeah, I said. *Got any ideas?*

Hell yes, girl. You have friends. In places.

I let out a sigh of exasperation. Apparently, cryptic communication ran in Lana's family. Why couldn't they just come right out and say what they meant?

Friends in places. I ran through my mental list.

There was Chuck. In the Greasy Rider Bike Shop. He had a bunch of keys—on his belt loop. Not the kind of key I needed here.

There was Lior. In Israel—no help there.

The Contessa. In her Boca palazzo. Her influence could open a lot of doors—metaphorical ones, not actual ones.

Leonard. Mom's live-in. Ex-CIA . . . he probably had a way . . .

Wait—of course—Enrique! As chief of security at the Boca Beach Hilton, he had a master magnetic key card that could override the code on any room in the hotel—or any other magnetic lock.

Okay, cool, I told Sylvester. *But how will I get a message to Enrique? There is a phone in my room . . .*

It could be bugged, Sylvester said.

I know that, I said with some irritation. Just like Lana, Sylvester also had a way of overstating the obvious. If I had my glass of Hennessy in hand, which I usually did when Lana showed up, it would take the edge off the interaction.

I rose from the lounge. *Well, nice to meet you, and thanks for your help, Sylvester*, I said.

Call me Slick, he said, and floated off with a flip of his teen-sized tail.

I went inside and found Mercy at the nurses' station. "I'm still waiting to get a call back about who can see you," she said.

"That's fine," I said. "In the meantime, I'd like to call a friend, but I don't have his number since you guys took my cell phone. Would you have a phone book I could borrow?"

"Sure." She looked under the counter. "That's funny. It's not here." She rummaged around. "I don't know what happened to it. Well, I can look up the number for you on the web."

"Okay. It's the Boca Beach Hilton."

She Googled it and jotted down the number for me.

"Thanks a lot," I said, and went back into my room, closing the door behind me.

I called the Hilton and asked for Enrique.

"Hold please," the receptionist said. It was a command, not a request.

I was transported into the Holding Zone—the Twilight Zone of the twenty-first century. That place you can never escape from, where you're at the mercy of those at the other end. It's probably where Rod Serling resides in the afterlife, chain-smoking as he chuckles over the fate of us mortals helplessly hanging on the line.

A series of beeps was periodically interrupted by a series of come-ons from a seductive female voice. "Thank you for calling the Boca Beach Hilton. Did you know you can make your reservation online and save time and money? Just go to <u>bocabeach.com</u>." *Beep. Beep. Beep.* "Take advantage of our stay-two-nights-get-one-free offer. Just go to . . ." *Beep. Beep. Beep.* "How about a Ladies Day at our world-class spa? Get a massage and facial for just $99.99. Go to . . ." *Beep. Beep. Beep.*

My nails were digging into the palms of my hands, and I was about to throw the receiver at the wall when Enrique finally came on.

"Hailey?" he said. He must have seen the caller ID from The Oasis and apparently had already been briefed by Leonard on my undercover identity. As I might have expected from the super-efficient super-spy. He had my back.

"Yes, it's me," I said. "Listen, I could really use a friend right now." I let out a sob for the benefit of anyone who might be listening in as I tried to think of a way to phrase my request. I knew Enrique could figure out what I needed if I just used the right code words.

"I'm feeling *trapped* in this place," I said. "I need help to *unlock* the demons that are driving me to drink," I said. "It's like they've got a *magnetic* pull on me. I think you might hold a *key* to solving this problem."

"I hear you," Enrique said. "I can be there in a half hour."

"Oh, thank you, sweetheart." I didn't typically use terms of endearment with him—or anyone, for that matter—but figured it would further my ruse if anyone was listening in.

I went back out to talk to Mercy at the nurses' station.

"My friend would like to visit," I said. "Can you please put him on the visitors list at the guard gate?"

"No problem."

"Thanks."

As soon as I returned to my room, I heard yelling outside the window. I walked over to look out and saw Hernandez and Fernandez dragging a handcuffed man toward a cop car. I recognized him as the Haitian gardener I had seen spraying the lawn with green liquid when I'd first arrived.

Through the glass windowpane I could hear his muffled shouts in French. *"Je n'ai rien fait! Je n'ai rien fait!"* I knew just enough of the language to translate: "I didn't do anything! I didn't do anything!"

Chapter 6

THROUGH THE window of my room, I watched Hernandez and Fernandez put the gardener in the back of a patrol car and drive off. For a moment I wanted to bang on the window and yell, "Stop!" But what purpose would that serve?

Certainly the gardener could have done it. He had the means—the hedge clippers—and the opportunity—he and the victim, Demarcus, both had access to the maze. As for motive, who knew? Had the gardener become enraged at Demarcus for stepping on his grass? Did the two of them have some prior relationship?

Maybe with the gardener's arrest, the crime was solved and I could check out. Of course, the police were never wrong. Yeah, right. Besides, what about the other two teens who had allegedly died before Demarcus? Had the police even looked into those rumors?

Since I was already on the inside, I might as well continue with my own investigation. If it turned out the gardener really was the killer of three victims, I wouldn't have lost much. Except a couple days of freedom. No Hog riding, no log cabin. Big sacrifices—but ones my Inner Vigilante was willing to make in pursuit of justice.

As I was contemplating, a knock came at the door. Upon opening it, I don't know who was more shocked, me or the woman who stood there. She was in her fifties, wearing a white embroidered peasant blouse and ruffled cotton skirt that brushed her ankles. Her salt and pepper hair was swept up on her head in elaborate braids. Large, intricate silver earrings and a matching necklace framed her face.

It was my old friend, Guadalupe Lourdes Fatima Domingo. Lupe for short. She was a Mexican-American anthropologist whom I had met on my first homicide case.

"Harr—" she started to say.

I grabbed her arm and pulled her inside, shutting the door behind her. I leaned in close, catching a scent of woodsy perfume. "We can't talk in here," I whispered in her ear. "Can we go outside?"

She leaned back and held me at arm's length, looking at me with her brows furrowed. "Yes, let's go," she said after a moment.

I guess she'd decided that I wasn't wacko. Or that if I was, she'd play along.

We stepped outside the room. Mercy, the nurse, sat at her station.

"Ms. . . . uh, Holloway and I are going to take a walk outside," Lupe told her.

"Sure," Mercy said. She rose, walked to the door of the suite, and unlocked it.

Lupe and I made our way down the hall, through the lobby, where Tiffani, the receptionist, smiled at us, and out onto the front lawn. I felt an immediate sense of relief at being sprung.

We sat on a wrought-iron bench overlooking a bed of bright pink and white flowers. The gardener's abandoned hose snaked through the grass.

We turned to each other. "What are you doing here?" we both asked simultaneously.

"I'm the chaplain," she said.

"But . . . but you're a witch," I said. I had witnessed some of her practices, like meditating in the moonlight, and she had told me a little about her beliefs involving communion with nature.

"*Bruja,*" she said.

"I know there's a big brouhaha going on here," I said. "But—"

"Not brouhaha. *Bruja.* A spiritual guide."

"Oh. But don't you have to be . . . I don't know, some mainstream religion to be a chaplain?"

"A chaplain can be of any faith and serve anyone—even nonbelievers. Here at The Oasis, the spiritual quest is all about recognizing one's Higher Power—however one may interpret that."

A large blue heron swooped down from the sky, landed at our feet, and proceeded to stare at us. If that was supposed to be some sign from a Higher Power, I had no idea what it meant. Lupe's presence still had me befuddled.

"You already have a job." I said. She was the executive director of a local rescue mission.

"This is a part-time consulting position. It gives me the opportunity to be of greater service to those in need."

"But you're a champion of the poor. What are you doing here with people who live in the lap of luxury?"

"Oh, Harriet," she said, gazing at the heron, who was now pecking at the grass. "You know the answer to that yourself. Those who are tied to material possessions are spiritually impoverished."

Of course she was right. I did know that very well.

"I guess I'm just shocked to see you here," I said.

"Likewise. I'm asked to conduct a spiritual assessment with a new client, Hailey Holloway, and instead I get Dirty Harriet."

"Please don't tell anyone, Lupe. I'm here undercover."

"I figured as much. Why?" she demanded.

I knew I could trust her. Besides, she could prove a big help to the investigation. So I told her about Gitta and how I'd ended up checking into The Oasis.

"I heard about Demarcus when I arrived," Lupe said. "It's tragic. Do you think there's a connection between his murder and the other two deaths?"

So the rumors were true—there had been two other deaths.

"I don't know," I said. "I need a couple days to investigate."

Lupe let out a breath. "Your being here really puts me in an ethical bind. If more children are in danger, I obviously want you to figure out what's going on. And I know you can. Will. On the other hand, I'm obligated to report your true identity to my colleagues."

"Why?" I asked. "Doesn't client confidentiality apply?"

"Only when it comes to revealing information to people outside the organization. But within the facility, we operate as a team. We have to share information among ourselves in order to provide coordinated treatment. If I deceive my colleagues, it will affect the entire team dynamics and patient care."

"But one of them—or more—could be killers," I said.

"Right," she sighed and was silent for a moment. Then she gripped my hand, intertwining our fingers. "I'm with you, sister," she said.

I squeezed her hand back.

"I'll tell the team that you declined chaplaincy services," Lupe said. "Which would be true. At least that will mitigate my ethical transgression somewhat."

"Awesome. Thanks, Lupe."

"But before I go, I do have to complete the spiritual assessment form. For the sake of appearances."

Damn. The prospect of having my spirit searched made me squirm. I wasn't used to being on the receiving end of probing questions. "Okay," I said with resignation.

Lupe pulled a sheet of paper and pen out of her large, multicolored woven bag.

"Harriet . . . I mean, Hailey, tell me what kind of religious up-bringing you had, if any."

As usual, I decided to follow my policy of sticking closely to the truth to minimize the possibility of being outed later by some inconsistency. "I'm a Jewaholic."

She blinked. "You're addicted to Jews?"

"No." At least I didn't think I was addicted to Lior. Was I? It was true that I was craving his return—was that a sign of a problem? Whatever. This was not the time to worry about that.

"Jewaholic," I repeated. "Half Jewish, half Catholic."

"I see," Lupe said.

"Mom is a cafeteria Catholic, and Dad was a Jewish atheist."

"What do you mean he 'was'?"

"He died when I was little. He was a traveling salesman, and one night up near Frostproof, Florida, he crashed headfirst into a Texas longhorn that had wandered onto the road. I guess it's good that he was an atheist, because the mix of meat and dairy that resulted wouldn't have been kosher."

Lupe looked at me for a moment before proceeding. "And what does the term 'cafeteria Catholic' mean to you?"

"Mom just picks and chooses what she wants from the catechism menu. For example, she believes in the sacrament of marriage. Really believes. I mean, she did it four more times after dad died. And is about to again, I think. On the other hand, she obviously has no problem with divorce."

"And your stepfathers? What kind of religious influence did they have on you?"

"They were all Jewish, too." If I wasn't addicted to Jews, Mom certainly was. Was there a treatment program for that?

"So what was it like growing up in an interfaith household?" Lupe asked.

"I couldn't say, since I have nothing to compare it to."

"Well, describe some of the traditions your family observed."

"Okay. Every week we'd observe two days of rest—Saturdays, per Jewish custom, and Sundays, per Christian custom. So not a damn thing got done on weekends. The whole family would just loaf around the pool."

"Uh-huh." Lupe scribbled some notes.

"Can you tell me anything about the teens who died here?" I asked.

She looked up from her notes, locking her gaze with mine. "Not ethically."

"You've already crossed that line," I said.

She sighed. "You don't let up, that's for sure. That's why I know you'll figure out what happened here. But let me finish this assessment first."

"Okay," I said. I guess I had to give some to get some.

"What else can you tell me about your family's customs?"

"Let's see . . . on Fridays during Lent, when Catholics aren't supposed to eat meat, Mom served gefilte fish. Then on Eastover, Mom and I would paint little bearded rabbis with yarmulkes onto Easter eggs. Then we'd eat matzo ball soup and chocolate bunnies."

"Okay. Go on."

"After Mom's first divorce, she was barred from communion in the church. So she got a lay Eucharistic minister to come to the house every week and give her communion. The wine was Manischewitz, and the wafers were bagel chips. Which I actually think is totally appropriate since the body and blood of Christ were Jewish."

"I see you have some interesting notions," Lupe said.

"Yeah. When I was fourteen, I missed my period for a couple months, and I was convinced I was pregnant. Although I'd never had sex. I mean, if it can happen to the Virgin Mary, it can happen to anyone, right? I figured I must be carrying the true Messiah."

Lupe's eyes widened. She was starting to look alarmed.

"Relax," I said. "I'm not delusional. Not anymore, anyway."

"Well, it sounds like your upbringing was a little . . . confusing."

"I suppose. I will say that when you pile original sin on top of your run-of-the-mill Jewish neuroses, it does make life kind of a bitch."

"How would you say your . . . uh . . . unorthodox childhood environment has shaped who you are today?"

I thought for a bit.

"You know what? I think it has actually made me a better investigator. Whoops, I guess you can't write that in your notes. But anyway, it's given me the ability to see many sides of an issue. I'm not blinded by a narrow dogmatic perspective." Damn. Guess I'd have to thank Mom for that.

Lupe scribbled some more, then looked up. "And what are your current views on spirituality? What do you think about a Higher Power?"

"What do you mean by 'Higher Power'?"

"Something greater than yourself. A source of wisdom, strength, guidance. That which gives your life meaning. A moral compass."

I thought about that a moment. Did I have a Higher Power? Something inside me poked at my ribs. Of course—my Inner Vigilante. That seeker of Truth and Justice. That was my Higher Power.

"Yeah," I said. "I can get on board with the Higher Power thing."

"Then that's the start of recovery."

And righteousness, I thought.

Lupe put her pen and paper away. "Well, that concludes the assessment." She rose.

The blue heron took flight, as if it, too, had concluded its mission. What was this bird, some kind of heavenly emissary? Whatever. Time to get to the hellish business at hand.

"So, about the kids here . . . ," I prompted.

"I really don't know much," she said. "Like I said, I just now found out about poor Demarcus. The other two died before I had a chance to meet with them. I don't always have the opportunity to speak with clients right away, like I did with you."

"But wouldn't you have been called in to do grief counseling with their families?"

"Normally, yes. But these were foster children. So was Demarcus. The foster care system handles contact with their parents."

"Oh," I said. That might explain Gardenia LaFleur's cry about her "children." Maybe she was their foster mother. She certainly seemed to be in need of grief counseling now. But more importantly . . . here was a connection among the dead.

"Isn't it strange that a whole group of foster kids would be in treatment for addiction?" I asked.

"Not at all. Sadly, foster kids are at high risk for addiction and all kinds of emotional and behavioral problems due to all the turmoil in their lives. And often feeling that they've been abandoned by their birth parents."

"Yeah, that's understandable," I said. "But what are the odds of three foster kids dying and it being a coincidence?"

"Just about zero, I'd say."

"Right. What are foster children doing at The Oasis, anyway? Wouldn't they be sent to a public treatment program?"

"Usually, yes. They're here due to the Contessa's beneficence."

Lupe knew the Contessa well, since the Contessa was also the benefactor of Lupe's rescue mission.

"The Contessa is funding five beds in the adolescent unit to be set aside for foster children with addictions," Lupe said. "Whenever there's an opening, whoever is first on the waiting list for the county facility gets in here."

"Oh."

The Contessa never spoke of her past, but it was rumored that she'd been a hidden child in World War II—a Jewish child living with a Christian family and passing as one of them. If that was true, I could see how she might feel an affinity for foster children, who also lived in a faux family.

Regardless of the Contessa's motivations, more foster kids at The Oasis meant more potential victims. "You need to let the Contessa know about these deaths."

"Yes, of course. I already have. About the first two, that is. But those weren't murders."

"What did they die of?" I asked.

"According to Dr. Stillwater, the first one, Angel Romero, had a seizure. That's not uncommon during withdrawal. But tragically, he was in the bathroom at the time and hit his head on the edge of the sink when he fell. Of course, when the staff found him, they immediately called an ambulance, and he was taken to the ER. But there was too much traumatic brain injury. He couldn't be revived."

"Wow. Sad," I said. "What about the other child?"

"Kenyatta Underwood. Fifteen years old. When she got here, she refused to eat. At first, the staff thought that would pass after the withdrawal phase. But after a few days, she still wasn't eating, and then her lab results came in, and it became clear she'd been anorexic for some time. Her electrolytes were totally out of whack. The staff was about to have her transferred to the hospital when she went into cardiac arrest."

So what Gitta had told me about one victim being poisoned and another suffocated were apparently unfounded rumors among the patients. Or maybe, in her coke-fueled paranoia, Gitta had twisted the facts. Certainly, I trusted Lupe's version of events over Gitta's. On the other hand, maybe Dr. Stillwater had lied to Lupe.

"There was no evidence of foul play in either of the cases?" I asked.

"Well, I don't think the possibility crossed anyone's mind."

"Right. But now with Demarcus's murder, and knowing that all of them were foster children, it kind of puts things in a new light."

Lupe nodded slowly.

"You said you didn't have a chance to meet with Angel and

Kenyatta, but what about Demarcus?"

"Yes, I was able to speak with him. He was a lovely young man. Extremely polite. Spiritually, he'd been raised in the African Methodist Episcopal church and was an avid member. He had a strong faith in God. In my opinion, he would have done very well in recovery. He just needed the support of a structured environment."

"Did he exhibit any unusual behaviors?" A standard question in murder investigations.

Lupe was silent for a while. "Well, he was extremely quiet. He said his favorite activity was reading. You know, that's pretty uncommon among kids his age. Normally it's video games, Facebook, all that."

"Hmm. Did he say what he liked to read?"

"He said everything. Science fiction, biographies—even romance."

"Whatever he could get his hands on?"

"I guess so."

"Did he mention any enemies? Any arguments he'd had with anyone?" More standard questions.

"No. Like I said, he had a very respectful demeanor. He wasn't the type I'd imagine getting into fights."

"He doesn't sound like a typical drug addict," I said.

"No, you're right."

"But he might have been the type that's a target of bullies," I said.

"That's true."

I sat for a while, thinking over what Lupe had shared. It was clear that she didn't know a lot of details about the victims. But she would know some generalities about The Oasis.

"How do things work here?" I asked. "Do the adult and adolescent patients mix?"

"Not much. Adults aren't allowed in the adolescent unit and vice versa. All the treatment sessions are conducted separately. But they do mix in the common areas, like the dining room and the outdoors."

Like the Meditation Maze, I thought.

"And what does the treatment involve?"

"The treatment plans are individualized for each patient. But in general, there are educational groups, therapy groups, individual counseling, family sessions, and mind-body work."

"And what do you think of the staff?"

"They're top-notch. You get what you pay for, just like with anything else. It shouldn't be that way when it comes to human pain and suffering, but it is. The treatment the kids get here, compared to what they'd get in the public facility, is like night and day. The clients here—or the Contessa—pay top dollar, and The Oasis hires the top people in the field. They're bright, skilled, and dedicated."

Perhaps, although not all were quite as dedicated as Lupe seemed to think. Dr. Stillwater, for one, seemed more dedicated to her annual Italian getaway.

A hiss erupted from the ground beneath us. *What the hell was that? A snake?* I jumped off the bench, just as water spurted out of sprinklers, spraying our way. We sprinted off the lawn onto the walkway.

Lupe took my hands. "I know you'll get to the bottom of whatever is going on here," she said. "Just be safe, *chica.*"

"I will. By the way—are the phones in this place bugged?"

"No. That would be an invasion of privacy. If anyone found out, the fallout would be a PR nightmare. I'm sure the execs wouldn't want that." She gave a crooked smile.

I wasn't entirely reassured.

Chapter 7

AS LUPE WALKED away, a midnight-blue BMW with tinted windows pulled into the parking lot. Enrique. He emerged and scanned his surroundings, like the security pro he was.

Seeing me, he strolled over.

He wore ivory silk pants and a baby-blue polo shirt with the collar turned up. A blue-and-white striped sweater tied around his neck completed the *GQ* look. His black hair was artfully gelled so that a few strands brushed the top of his Ray-Bans. He was the only guy I knew who could look completely cool on a sultry South Florida day.

We sat down on a bench that was out of reach of the sprinklers. "What's with the rinky-dink rent-a-cop at the gate?" he asked.

I shrugged. Pros of any kind always had to pass judgment on each other. Bakers did it, bankers did it. Hell, I guess even the birds and the bees did it. I could just see one bee talking to another: "Miss Queen Bee over there thinks she's all that. We do all the work, and she takes all the credit."

"I know, right?" the other bee says.

Enrique turned to me and lowered his sunglasses so they hung beneath his chiseled chin. What the hell had started this trend of dangling the glasses off the ears instead of propping them atop the head? His brown eyes looked into mine. "Are you safe?" he asked. "Do you need backup?"

My first instinct was to say, "I can take care of myself." But that would be an insult to the relationship Enrique and I had developed over the years. I had to face the facts. Yes, I could take care of myself. But I didn't have to push friends away. I didn't have to prove my independence anymore.

"I'm being careful," I said. "If I need help, I'll call. I already have, right?"

"Yeah. Okay, I won't ask what's going on. I know you'll tell me if I need to know." He clapped his hands on his knees. "I'm sorry, but I can't stay. I've got to head back to the hotel. There's a convention of high school principals going on. Man, the way those people party, you'd think they were kids themselves."

"Maybe they are," I said. "Eternal kids. I mean, who would voluntarily choose to be in a high school?" The memory of my own high school, with its cliques and castes, made me cringe. Principals were probably the Queen Bees still climbing over each other to become Prom Queen.

Enrique stood up.

"But wait, what about the magnetic k—" I started to say as I rose, but Enrique reached out, encircled my waist, and pulled me to him, hard. Then he kissed me full on the lips, and his hands glided down to my ass.

What the hell? Enrique was gay. He was married to Chuck, my BFF. Even if Enrique had decided to expand his sexual repertoire, there was no way I was going to be a party to a betrayal. I uttered a muffled protest and pushed on his chest. I was about to shove a knee into his groin when he let go and backed away.

"See ya," he said with a wink and a smile.

I collapsed back on the bench in befuddlement. As I did, something poked me in the ass. I reached around and felt my back pocket. Something thin and hard was in it. I pulled it out. It was the magnetic key card.

I walked back into the building. The receptionist, Tiffani, escorted me to the detox unit and unlocked the door for me. Mercy looked up from the nurses' station. "Oh, I'm glad you're back, Hailey. It's dinnertime. I need to take your vital signs, then I'll show you to the cafeteria."

This was a positive development. I'd been thinking I'd be stuck in my room, unable to act until nighttime. But now I might have the opportunity to interrogate some of the patients.

After Mercy recorded my temperature, blood pressure, pulse, and respiration rate, I followed her down several hallways into a large, glass-enclosed solarium. Potted palms and ferns reached for the sky. Round, wrought-iron café tables and chairs were scattered among the foliage.

I recognized the group of water nymphs seated at one large table together with their instructor, Miss Sea World. The male T'ai Chi masters and their staff leader, Sandy, were at another. There were no empty chairs at either table. Three smaller, four-top tables were similarly occupied.

At the opposite end of the room, two girls and two boys sat at another four-top. They all looked to be fifteen or sixteen years old. One of the girls sported dyed-red dreadlocks and tattoos that ran the lengths of her skinny white arms. The other had spiky black hair and multiple ear, nose, and lip piercings. Both wore print sundresses, the cheap kind that have irregular white streaks where the fabric was folded as it went through printing production in some overseas sweatshop.

In contrast, one of the two brown-haired boys wore a Ralph Lauren polo shirt and skinny jeans, while the other boasted an Abercrombie T-shirt and plaid longboard shorts. However, all four kids wore flip-flops—that great Florida leveler. In Boca, you'd never know someone's social class by looking at their feet. However, from the rest of their attire, I guessed the girls were members of the foster care population while the boys were pampered Boca preppies.

The girls talked with each other, gesturing with their hands as they sipped from Coke bottles. The boys slouched in their seats, drinking Gatorade and looking bored. I wondered what the girls were talking about and why the boys didn't seem to care. I needed to be at that table . . . but I would obviously not belong.

"Harr . . . Hailey!" I heard Gitta's voice and turned to see her waving wildly at me from a small corner table. She was with a teenage boy who was dressed similarly to those at the other table.

"Oh good," Mercy said. "I see you have someone to sit with. Enjoy your meal." She departed.

I'd wanted to sit with some of the other patients in hopes of gleaning new information, but all the other seats were occupied. So I walked over to Gitta's table.

The boy rose and held an empty chair out for me. On closer inspection, I recognized him as Lars, Gitta's son of about seventeen, whom I'd previously encountered a few times. He had the tall, blond, blue-eyed Scandinavian features of his mother. And I remembered his impeccable manners. Despite her problems, Gitta, or perhaps her kids' father, had managed to raise well-behaved children.

"Nice to see you again, Ms. Holloway," Lars said, holding out his hand.

Gitta darted her eyes left and right. "Lars is visiting," she whispered. "I've told him everything."

That seemed like a lot to lay on a kid. But then, Lars had probably been the adult in their relationship for quite some time. After all, the "Babe" in "Boca Babe" didn't refer only to a woman's looks.

"Where are your other two kids?" I asked as Lars and I sat down.

"They're home with the nanny," Gitta said. "I think they're too young to be in this environment."

Wow, she was starting to show some mature judgment.

Gitta pulled on a strand of her long hair and twisted it around her finger. "So what's going—" she started to whisper, but cut herself off when a young man, clad in a white shirt and apron with black pants and tie, approached.

Wait—a waiter? In here? Okay, okay, I should have known—this was Boca.

"My name is Jason, and I'll be your server this evening." He held out a leather-bound menu. "I apologize we only have one menu, so you'll have to share. For some reason, they've all been disappearing. What can I get you to drink?"

"I'll have an Arnold Palmer, please," Gitta said.

That sounded borderline obscene. Or alcoholic. I raised my eyebrows at Gitta.

"Don't look at me like that," she said. "It's just lemonade and iced tea."

"Oh." That sounded pretty good. "I'll have that, too," I said.

Jason turned to Lars. "And for you? The same?"

"No thanks, I don't do caffeine. I'll have some coconut water, please."

Coconut water? Sure, every restaurant had that in stock. But Jason didn't blink an eye. "Coming right up."

"So what have you found out?" Gitta pounced as soon as Jason left.

I glanced around the dining area. The water nymphs were giggling, and the T'ai Chi masters were high-fiving each other about something. The two teen girls were still in intense discussion, leaning toward each other, while the boys sat back, silent. No one seemed remotely interested in our conversation.

In low tones, I quickly filled Gitta and Lars in on what I knew so far. When I told them that the deaths of the first two teens were reportedly non-homicidal, Gitta insisted, "But all the other patients say they were murdered."

"I'm not saying they weren't. I'm merely objectively reporting to you, as my client, the information I've uncovered as your investigator." Okay, maybe I said it a little testily.

"She's right, Mom," Lars said. "Further investigation will be needed to reconcile this apparent discrepancy in the manners of death."

The kid sounded a little nerdy. Worse, he sounded more than a little eager. Was he angling to assist in said investigation? I hoped not. The last thing I needed was an adolescent apprentice.

Jason arrived with our drinks. "Have you decided what you'd like to eat?" he asked.

"Oh, I'm sorry, we haven't looked at the menu yet," Gitta said.

"I'll give you a moment," Jason said and left.

Lars held the menu in the middle of the table so that all three of us could peer at it.

Appetizers
Prosciutto-wrapped grilled asparagus
Corn and crab fritters
Yellow bean salad with marinated mushrooms

Entrées
Miso-glazed sea bass
Veal chop Milanese
Roasted squab

Desserts
Fresh strawberries with Chantilly cream
Warm pear cobbler with vanilla bean gelato
Chocolate fondant layer cake with caramel sauce

Wow. Culinary choices like these were typical fare for Boca Babes. But those foster kids must have thought they'd died and gone to heaven.

I caught myself mid-thought in shame. Some of them *had* died, for Chrissake.

When Jason returned, Gitta ordered the asparagus and sea bass, and I went for the fritters and veal chop.

Lars said, "I'm sorry to be a bother, but do you have any vegan choices?"

"Sure," Jason said. "We have Portobello tacos with chipotle salsa, mock meatloaf with scallion pancakes, and tofurkey burger on a twelve-grain bun with an Asian fusion salad."

Asian fusion? What the hell was that? Did he mean Confucian? Clearly, I was in a state of confusion.

Lars, apparently, was not. "I'll have the tacos," he said. "Thanks."

Jason departed. Gitta smiled at her son and told me, "Lars is a health food enthusiast."

As if I hadn't detected that already, ace PI that I am. I thought for a moment. I sure didn't want Lars as an investigative assistant, but maybe he could be a source. "Do you know anything about teen drug use in

Boca?" I asked him.

"My son is not—" Gitta started to say.

I cut her off. "I'm not saying he is. I'm just asking if he knows anything."

"It's intense," Lars said. "At least at my school."

Gitta stared at him.

"What school do you go to?" I asked.

"Boca Country Day."

My own high-priced alma mater. The private tuition had been generously sponsored by my stepdad No. 4, Mortimer Rosenberg, owner of Mort's Mortuary chain, whom Mom had snagged when I was fifteen.

The drugs of choice back in my day had been booze, roofies, and Ecstasy. Not that I ever partook . . . okay, maybe once or twice. But I'd quickly realized I didn't like losing control. Of course, I still enjoyed my daily glass of Hennessy. In fact, right about now was the time for it. I took a sip of my Arnold Palmer. Nice. But it didn't quell my craving.

"So, what do you mean, it's intense?" I asked Lars.

"The competition. We've all got to get into the top colleges, right?"

"Lars's first choice is MIT," Gitta interrupted, patting him on the shoulder. "Harvard is his safety school."

"Uh-huh," I said. "So if kids are doing drugs, how can they expect to get into those places?"

"You're thinking the wrong kinds of drugs," Lars said. "I'm talking performance-enhancing pills."

"Like what?"

"Ritalin. Adderall."

"What are those?"

"Stimulants. They're prescribed for attention deficit disorder. But if you don't have ADD and you take them, your brain power skyrockets. You get ultra-focus and energy. You can pull all-nighters and ace exams."

"Lars, are you saying you use these . . . ?" Gitta asked.

Lars rolled his eyes. I guess he had some typical teenage traits after all. "No, Mom. I inherited *Dad's* brains."

Gitta didn't seem to take this as an insult to her own intelligence.

I just hoped the kid hadn't also inherited his father's morals. The late Lapidus O'Malley, Gitta's first husband, had been the sleaze-ball founding partner of the law firm that Bruce had worked in. They defended big companies against lawsuits brought by families who'd lost loved ones due to corporate malfeasance. Like pharmaceutical companies who knowingly sold meds with deadly side effects. Speaking of which . . .

"So these pills," I said. "How do kids get them?"

"Dealers," Lars said matter-of-factly. "There are a few kids who get prescriptions from their doctors, then they sell the pills to the other students."

Just then, yells erupted from the other side of the solarium. I looked over. The commotion was at the teens' table. The two girls were tugging on a half-empty Coke bottle.

"Gimme that, Amber, you bitch!" Red Dreadlocks yelled.

"Screw you, Jessica!" Black Spikes screamed.

Dreadlocks pulled the bottle out of Spikes' grasp and gulped the contents.

I stood up and started to head over to intervene.

Gitta gripped my arm. "No, *Hailey*," she said, with emphasis. "Don't call attention to yourself."

Out of the corner of my eye I saw the staff—Jason, Sandy, and Miss Sea World—running toward the table.

"Amber! Jessica! Stop it!" Miss Sea World yelled.

But before any of us could reach it, Black Spikes picked up a fork, raised it over her head, and stabbed the tines into Red Dreadlocks' neck.

Chapter 8

SCREAMS ERUPTED throughout the dining room as blood spurted from Jessica's neck. I ran over, reaching the girl before the staffers did. I grabbed a linen napkin from her table, and kneeling down to where she lay on the floor, pressed it to the wound, where the fork was embedded. The girl's freckled face was pale, her eyes glassy.

Sandy and Miss Sea World restrained Amber, who seemed to be lunging for the disputed bottle.

"We need medical help!" Sandy said. "Where's Dr. Stillwater?"

"She's left for the day," Miss Sea World said. "Jason, call the detox nurse, Mercy," she told the waiter, who whipped out his phone.

The other diners all gathered around the scene in a circle, screaming, grabbing each other, and generally acting useless.

We needed more than medical help—we needed the cops. "Somebody call 911!" I yelled.

The patients stood rooted like trees. It felt like a replay of that afternoon when Gitta and I had found Demarcus stabbed in the Meditation Maze. Finally, Gitta's son, Lars, pulled out a phone, punched in the numbers, and relayed the information.

The napkin I held to the girl's throat was now soaked with blood. When Lars hung up, he handed me another one. As I switched them, a squirt of blood streaked onto my chest. The girl's breathing became shallow and irregular, and her eyes rolled back in her head.

"Hold on, Jessica," I told her. "Help is coming. You're going to be fine."

I soon heard pounding footsteps as the nurse arrived, followed shortly by the paramedics and police. I felt arms pulling me away. Then I watched, strangely detached, as if I were seeing a movie, as the medical personnel administered first aid to Jessica and the cops handcuffed Amber. Then they swooped the victim and the assailant to their respective holding cells, the hospital and the jail.

I was left sitting on the floor, my hands and chest covered in blood, a throng of people surrounding me. The sensations, the smell, the stickiness—suddenly I was no longer in the dining room of The Oasis.

I'M IN THE ballroom of the Boca Raton Beach Club. I've just shot Bruce with his own gun, in the middle of a friend's wedding reception, as he'd been about to strike me with his fist. Blood is spattered on my chest, my face. It feels hot, smells metallic. I'm surrounded by people in a cocoon of silence. Then screams erupt. From them. And from me.

"Hailey! Hailey!" Someone was shaking my shoulder. Slowly my consciousness came back to the present, and I saw Mercy, the nurse, gazing into my eyes.

"What?" I looked at my hands, saw the blood, noticed that it had seeped under my fingernails, pooling there. Looking back up, I saw the other patients staring at me, immaculate in their designer duds.

Mercy reached a hand to me. "Let's get you up. I know this has been a traumatic experience."

No. Shooting Bruce had been my real traumatic experience. This was like an aftershock to an earthquake. I brushed away Mercy's hand and struggled to my feet.

Dammit, I'd thought I was over the post-traumatic stress—the nightmares, the flashbacks like the one I'd just had. Would it never end? Maybe I did need help.

Nah. I needed Hennessy. Or my Hog.

The staff, though, seemed to think we all needed help. "We're going to have a trauma debriefing for all the patients in half an hour," Mercy said. "So let's get you cleaned up, and then we'll come back here."

She escorted me to a restroom, where she instructed me to wash with disinfectant soap. As if I couldn't figure that out myself. She said she'd be right back, and a few minutes later she returned, carrying a form-fitting pink polo shirt with "The Oasis" embroidered on the upper right.

"It's from the gift shop," she said.

Of course. Just like any other high-priced hotel. No doubt the cost would appear on my—or rather, Gitta's—bill.

I changed tops and threw my old one into the trash. Even if the bloodstains would come out, I didn't want the reminder.

We went back to the dining atrium, which was now full of people, all jabbering simultaneously, like birds of different species each singing its own tune. The table and floor where the stabbing had happened were wiped clean. The smell of disinfectant hung in the air.

Gitta and Lars occupied the same table we had earlier, and Gitta waved me over. She bombarded me with questions before I even had a chance to sit. "What's going on? Is that girl—Jessica—going to be all right?"

As I sat, a microphone emitted one of those ear-splitting squeals. The room went silent as people cringed and covered their ears.

"Sorry about that, everyone," a voice said. It was Dr. Stillwater, evidently having returned to the facility to deal with the crisis. She stood on a platform at the front of the room. "If I may have your attention, please." She waited a moment, then continued. "We've all had a very difficult day here at The Oasis. As I'm sure you've all heard by now, we sadly lost a member of The Oasis family, Demarcus Pritchard."

The woman seemed to be a master of understatement. *Difficult day? Sadly lost?* How about a day from hell with a vicious murder?

"And a short time ago," Dr. Stillwater continued, "we had an incident here in our dining area resulting in injury to a young lady, Jessica Jarrett. But I want everyone to know that you are safe. The police have arrested the two individuals responsible for these incidents, so I am confident the matters are resolved."

Murmurs went around the room. "Yeah, right," I heard. "So you say." It sounded like she had failed to reassure the restless inmates. Including me.

As far as I was concerned, nothing was resolved. What was the real cause of the girls' fight? There had to be more to it than a simple conflict over a Coke. And was it connected to the murder of Demarcus and the deaths of the other two teens?

"Now, at times like this," the doctor continued, "it's very normal to feel anxious. These events may have re-traumatized many of you, brought back unpleasant memories from your past."

Now heads were nodding. Including, I noticed, my own. *Stop it,* I told myself. I didn't need to be sucked into this psychobabble.

"Those of you who have been with us a while here at The Oasis know that one of our guiding principles is that we all must recognize and get in touch with our feelings," the doctor said.

Oh, gag me.

"It's normal at times like this to crave a return to old using habits. After all, that is how people with addictions deal with feelings—by repressing them with mood-altering substances. So today presents us with an opportunity to practice newfound skills. I would like to invite anyone who would care to share their feelings to do so now."

Not only was she a master of understatement, but of reframing, too. Murder was not an atrocity. It was an opportunity. And someone was seizing it; a hand went up in the middle of the room, and the microphone was passed. The hand belonged to one of the T'ai Chi men from that afternoon, a buff guy in his thirties. He wore shorts, and for the first time, I saw that he had a metal prosthesis in place of his right leg.

"When I saw that boy lying dead on the ground today," he said, "it took me right back to Iraq, the day my best buddy was killed by friendly fire."

The room went even more silent than it had already been.

"My life was never the same after that," the man said. "Sure, I've been successful, made a lot of money since then . . . but it's like some part of me died that day too, you know what I'm saying?"

"You're right, Kyle," Dr. Stillwater said. "A part of you did die. That hole in your heart will always be there. But with time and support, you'll learn to live again. Your life won't be the same, but it will be a life worth living."

Heads nodded again, and a murmur of support went around the room like a wave.

Gitta raised her hand, and Kyle passed the mike to her.

"Um . . . the way those two pretty young girls were fighting over the Coke bottle," she said, ". . . it reminded me of the way contestants treated each other in the beauty pageants I was in. Fights broke out all the time, girls pulling each other's hair and gouging each other's faces." She stopped as a lump moved down her throat. "But that wasn't the worst part of it. When I was in the Miss Universe pageant, um . . . one of the judges raped me."

I heard a few gasps.

Gitta twisted her hair around her finger. "That was the way it was back then," she said. "You had to put up with it if you wanted to win. If you told anybody, they'd blame you, saying you made him do it, you didn't know how to behave properly." She stopped again and took a few trembling breaths. "I've never told anybody about it until now."

Wow. No, she sure had never told me about it. I was starting to see her in a different light.

"That took a lot of courage for you to share, Gitta," Dr. Stillwater said. "And now that you have, you can start the healing process."

Gitta nodded, still pulling on her hair, and passed the mike to a thin woman who slumped in her chair, her stringy hair obscuring her face.

"I feel so sorry for that murdered boy's mother," the woman said.

"I lost my son when he was five."

"Renee, it sounds like you're turning a corner in your recovery process," Dr. Stillwater said. "You're able to see others' pain. Your own may not be as overwhelming as it once was."

"I think you're right, Dr. Stillwater," Renee said.

Hmm. I had to give Stillwater credit. She did seem to be skilled in responding to the patients, despite what I took as her earlier insensitive statements—including the gripe I'd overheard that afternoon about the teens' deaths potentially disrupting her Italian vacation plans. Lupe had told me the staff was topnotch, and maybe she was right. That didn't preclude them from having human faults.

A few more patients told their testaments of trauma. After about an hour, Dr. Stillwater cut them off. "It's getting late, but I want to thank you all for sharing. It's important for each of us to know that we're not alone, that there are others who have had similar experiences. Now we'd like everyone to go back to their units, and remember, the staff is always available to talk if you need to."

I sat for a moment amid the commotion as chairs scraped and people rose. I had a strange feeling that I couldn't pinpoint.

Gitta and Lars rose.

"Oh my God, I'm so terrified," Gitta said. "I can't face spending the night in here."

"You'll be fine, Mom," Lars said. "Like the doctor said, the perpetrators have been apprehended."

I wasn't convinced of that. There had been too many fatal incidents to be coincidental. Something deeper had to be going on. However, I didn't want to upset Gitta further. And I still didn't think she was in danger. I reminded her that all the victims had been teenagers, and adults didn't seem to be targeted.

"All right," Gitta finally acceded. "Will I see you here at breakfast?"

"Yeah, I'll see you then."

She and Lars took off, and Mercy escorted me back to the Total Detoxification Purification unit. I still didn't see any other patients in the unit, nor had any come there from the dining room. I guess it was just me.

"How are you feeling now?" Mercy said.

"Edgy."

"Are you having cravings?"

"Yep."

"Here's what I'd like you to do. When you get a craving, take some deep breaths, count to ten, and tell yourself that it will pass. And it will. But if it does become unbearable, or you get any symptoms like sweating or difficulty breathing, just let me know, okay?"

"Okay," I said. The thought of being trapped in my room started to produce those very symptoms. "Can I go sit out on the patio?"

"Of course."

I went out and laid down on one of the chaise lounges. The sun had set, and moonlight reflected off the tranquil pond. It was a relaxing setting, but some feeling deep inside kept nagging at me, and I still couldn't figure out what it was.

The surface of the water rippled, and a pair of black eyeballs emerged. Slick was back.

Hey, he said.

Hey, yourself.

Whaddup?

I shrugged. *I don't feel like talking.*

He waved his tail and propelled himself closer to me. *Lana says when you're like this, something's bothering you big time.*

Oh, jeez. Just leave me alone, you prying predator, I said.

You're projecting, he said. *You're really angry at yourself, but you don't want to face that, so you're displacing it onto me.*

Is that so, Dr. Freud? And what, may I ask, am I angry at myself for?

For the attitude you've had about the people here. You've got a chip on your shoulder about Boca. You think we're all a bunch of fake flakes in this town. But when you heard people tell their stories tonight, you realized that underneath the fakeness and the flakiness there are actual human beings who are hurting. So you're a little ashamed about the way you've passed judgment.

Human beings? In Boca? Me, ashamed? Give me a break, I said.

Okay, he said, and dove underwater with a slight splash.

Damn him. He was just like his great-aunt. Always right.

Chapter 9

I WASN'T ABOUT to sit around ruminating over my harsh judgments of Boca's dissipated denizens. Just because Slick had taken up residence on the grounds of the asylum didn't make him the resident psychoanalyst. Anyway, I wasn't there for my mental health. I was there to find Truth and Justice.

Darkness had fallen, and it was time to implement my computer break-in plan. I hoped I could access the teens' patient records and look for commonalities that might tie their deaths together—and thus point to a viable suspect.

I left the patio and went back into my room, leaving the door open a crack. I could see Mercy at the nurses' station as I sat on the bed and looked into the mirror above the dresser. If she left, I could walk to the door and see if she was out of the area so that I could escape from the Total Purification Detoxification Unit.

Unfortunately, she stayed rooted in place, clacking at her keyboard and clicking her mouse, sounding like a woodpecker tapping a tree. What could she be doing? As far as I could tell, I was the only patient in the unit. Surely she didn't have all that much to write about me. She was probably Facebooking, Tweeting, Pinning, Instagramming, YouTubing, Flickring, Tumblring, Yelping, Linking In, or otherwise doing God knows what other time-sucking activity. It amazed me that some members of society worried about a potential zombie invasion when the Internet had already eaten the brains of most of the American population.

Finally, she rose and strode away from her station. I skedaddled to the door and saw her walk out onto the patio and light a cigarette. I slipped out of my room and booked for the door of the suite.

Before I reached it, I heard her call, "Hailey!"

I froze in my tracks and kept a rigid smile on my face as I turned to her.

"How are you doing?" she asked.

"Me? Um, fine. Fine. Just, uh, stretching my legs."

"Good," she said. She took a drag on her cigarette, then flicked it into the pond. I hoped it didn't hit Slick.

"Well, back to work," she said.

Yeah, right.

I retreated back into my room. Another half-hour passed before Mercy rose again. This time I watched her enter the restroom.

I slipped out of my room again, leaving the door ajar exactly as it had been so as not to arouse attention, and ran for the exit. I slid Enrique's master magnetic key through the slot. A click sounded, and I pushed the door open. Freedom!

The long hallway was empty, lined with closed office doors.

I figured that the facility's computers were networked, since all the staff would need access to the patient records and other shared data. Thus, Paula Green's login information should work on any of the units—I hoped. I tried the nearest office door, which was Dr. Stillwater's. The same room Hernandez had interviewed me in earlier.

The magic key worked again, and with a sigh of relief, I was in. In the darkness, I made out the desk in the far corner. I groped my way over to it, knocking over a wastebasket, hitting my shin on the coffee table, and letting out a few choice expletives along the way.

At last, I settled my ass into Stillwater's buttery-soft leather chair. I set my hand on the armrest. The whole thing started vibrating, sending me upright with a jolt.

What the hell?

I turned to look at the freaky furniture. In the dim light I could see the back of the chair rolling as if some demon were trying to escape. The damn thing was possessed . . . no, it was one of those automatic massage chairs.

Why was I surprised? This was Boca. Every self-respecting, upper-level manager must have had one.

As for me, I preferred the vibe of my Hog any day.

I stabbed at random buttons on the armrest, and the thing went through a jumble of gyrations before I finally landed on the "Stop" button and the whole throne went still. I deposited my butt again, this time keeping my arms locked at my sides.

My knees bumped the computer tower underneath the desk. I felt for the power button with my fingers and pressed it. The monitor came to life with a burst of sound and color courtesy of Microsoft's minions. After all the beeps, whirls, and swirls subsided, I was confronted with a demand for a username and password.

I conjured up the mental image I'd formulated when observing Paula Green's login. Two green bobcats, each with a huge rhinestone "98" swinging from a fat gold chain around its neck. I entered "green" as the username and "bobcats98" as the password.

The computer emitted a rude beep and flashed a bold red message: "Invalid username or password." *Shit.* What had I done wrong? Should "green" have been "greene?" I couldn't remember. I tried it with the same password. I got the same reply, this time with an additional warning: "You have one more try before system lockout."

I felt like kicking the damn thing. I had to get into those records. I took a deep breath and typed "Green" and "Bobcats98." The monitor transmuted into a set of icons set against a background image of a desert oasis. *Yesss!* I was in. Apparently, my keen powers of observation had missed Paula's pinkie hitting the shift key as she typed the initial letters of the two words.

An image of a medical chart loomed on the screen amid the usual Office Suite icons. My keen investigative acumen led me to deduce that this was the electronic medical record. I clicked it, and sure enough, a window opened asking me to search by patient name or ID. I typed in "Demarcus Pritchard." A slew of tabs popped up: "Patient Demographics;" "History & Physical;" "Psychosocial Assessment;" "Spiritual Assessment;" "Psychological Tests;" "Treatment Plan;" and "Progress Notes."

Damn, I didn't have all night. Mercy had said she would check my vital signs every four hours; the last had been at 6:00, so the next would be at 10:00. I needed to be back in my room by then. I looked at the digital clock in the lower right corner of the monitor. 9:17. Not enough time to go through all the records. So what would yield the most useful information? Who knew?

I clicked "History & Physical." That brought up a report filled with medical gobbledygook—a lot of sound and fury, signifying nothing to me. I tried "Psychosocial Assessment." Another long report popped up with headings: Presenting Problem . . . Personal Status . . . Drug History and Pattern of Use . . .

I scanned the report. "Patient is a 16-year-old African-American male who appears his stated age . . . Dress and hygiene are appropriate . . . oriented to time, place, and person . . . Speech is rapid in fluency . . . Patient presents with symptoms of social withdrawal, insomnia, and hyperactivity . . . Symptoms are suggestive of drug withdrawal . . . Patient denies past or current drug or alcohol use . . . Diagnosis deferred pending lab results . . ."

I clicked on "Lab Results." A column on the left listed alcohol, amphetamines, barbiturates, benzodiazepines, cannabis, cocaine, opiates, and phencyclidine. To the right of each was a single abbreviation: NEG.

Demarcus had tested negative for alcohol and all other drugs? That was odd. Shouldn't something have come up positive?

I went back to the "Home" screen and entered the name of one of the two other dead teens, Angel Romero. His lab results were the same: all negative. His psychosocial assessment was nearly identical to Demarcus's, with the exception that his presenting symptoms included seizures. His diagnosis was likewise deferred. The psych evaluator apparently used a boilerplate write-up, just plugging in symptoms, which were then incorporated into the computer-generated report.

I found the same results for the third teen, Kenyatta Underwood. Negative lab results coupled with symptoms of social withdrawal, lack of appetite, and aggressive behavior.

What the hell was going on here? All these kids had symptoms of drug withdrawal, yet there were no traces of drugs in their systems.

I needed to find out how long the various drug metabolites would show up in blood and urine samples. I Googled "How long do drugs stay in your system?" A list of sites came up. Along the side of the screen, a banner ad crept into my field of vision: "The *National Inquisitor.* Subscribe today! Only $1.95 per issue!"

Ignoring the ad, I clicked on the first search result, PassYour-DrugScreen.com. It told me that alcohol would be undetectable within one to twelve hours; most of the other drugs would not leave a trace after one to three days, with a few exceptions like marijuana, which might stay in the system a while longer.

Hmmm . . . so it appeared that none of the dead teens had used any drugs, with the possible exception of alcohol, within days prior to checking into the Oasis. Why not? Wouldn't addicts admitted into treatment usually be regular, probably daily, users? I thought of Gitta and Bruce. They'd both snorted every day. And I'd known plenty of alcohol addicts in my Boca Babe days; they, too, had had their daily Happy Hour, or twenty-four.

As I sat there pondering, the *Inquisitor* ad popped up again, this time flashing at me in orange and yellow. "Get a free gift for subscribing today!"

Suddenly I heard the click of a magnetic key in the office door. Oh no. Had Dr. Stillwater returned to her office? At this time of night?

I was busted. Wait . . . maybe not. I hit the monitor's power button to shut off its tell-tale glow, then wedged my body underneath the desk, concealing myself between it and the corner of the room. Beneath the back panel of the desk, I could see a slice of light as the office door opened. Then the overhead lights came on.

My heart pounded. I forced myself to breathe slowly and silently.

There was a shuffling of feet, then a loud grinding sound that made me start and hit my head on the top of the desk. *Shit.* A vacuum cleaner. It was the housekeeping staff. I crouched there, cramped, as the sound alternately approached and receded.

The repetitive reverberation was kind of like the trance-inducing repetition of a Harley engine. It propelled my mind into a familiar altered state. Which spawned a thought: didn't banner ads typically pop up in response to cookies left from prior searches? Had Dr. Stillwater been reading the *Inquisitor* online on her office computer?

The vacuum cleaner was shut off, and I heard paper rustling as the wastebasket was apparently picked up and emptied. *Hurry up*, I thought. *I need to get the hell out of here.*

A pair of white Croc-clad feet came underneath the desk as objects were moved atop it, and a swishing sound indicated dusting. Finally the feet retreated, the overhead lights went off, and the door clicked shut.

I started to untwist myself from my pretzel position. Damn, that hurt. My approaching fortieth wasn't looking too appealing at the moment.

After resuming my seat in the leather vibrator and turning the monitor back on, I checked the time. Less than twenty minutes before Mercy would come to my room.

I clicked on the machine's search history. Sure enough, there it was. The *Inquisitor* had been accessed that very morning, at 9:53 a.m. Another click brought up the page that had been viewed.

"Hot Mess Jordan Mitchell in Rehab!" a headline blared.

"Former Nickelodeon darling Jordan Mitchell, the now 17-year-old child star of *Friends & Family*, has entered rehab at The Oasis, the celeb drying-out spa in Boca Raton, Florida. The troubled teen reportedly checked herself in following an intervention staged by her father, renowned country singer Jay Mitchell, best known for his nineties hit, *Jaywalkin' on a Dead-End Street*."

A grainy photo of a thin young woman accompanied the gossip piece. Personally, I wouldn't have known her from Adam's housecat, but the caption assured me it was the starlet in question. And it said the picture was from the adolescent unit.

I glanced at the clock on the monitor. 9:50. I had a few more minutes left to snoop.

I looked at the search history again and saw that the *Inquisitor* had also been accessed a week previously. That would have been before the deaths of the other two teens.

The page on that date read, "Cody Keys Locked Up in Lux Detox." According to the accompanying story, the adolescent singing idol (news to me) was in The Oasis following violation of his probation for possession of marijuana. Another grainy photo, again purportedly from the adolescent unit, showed a kid in baggy pants and backward ball cap.

I glanced again at the clock. 9:55. I had no time to ponder what all this meant. I had to get back into my room before Mercy came and found me missing.

I shut off the computer and rose. Then I abruptly sat again. *Shit.* I'd forgotten one small detail—how would I get back into the detox unit without Mercy seeing me?

Chapter 10

TRYING TO COME up with a plan to sneak back into my room, I glanced around Dr. Stillwater's office. By the phone, I saw a list of facility numbers. Okay, I got it.

Using the speakerphone so I wouldn't have to leave the handset off the hook, I punched in the number for the detox unit nurses' station. I figured the caller ID on the other end would display Stillwater's name. I heard a few rings, then Mercy answered. "Hello?"

I made a choking noise.

"Is that you, Dr. Stillwater?" Mercy asked, sounding alarmed.

I rushed out of Stillwater's office, shut the door behind me, and plastered myself against the wall outside the door of the detox unit. As I'd hoped, Mercy opened the door, which swung outward, concealing me behind it. She ran past me to Stillwater's office, then I slipped into the detox unit as I heard her knock on Stillwater's door and say, "Dr. Stillwater? Are you in there?"

I let the detox door close behind me, took a few quick steps into my room, and closed that door. Safe. Mercy would probably call someone to check out Stillwater's office, but there'd be no reason for suspicion to fall on me.

I sat on my bed in the dark, pondering. Someone was obviously leaking confidential information to the *Inquisitor*, perhaps taking photos with a clandestine cell phone. It was also clear that The Oasis management was obsessed with maintaining the facility's reputation for discretion among the rich and famous.

Had Dr. Stillwater suspected—or discovered—that the adolescents were the source of the leaks? Would she go so far as to kill them to silence them? Supposedly, Angel Romero had died of a seizure and Kenyatta Underwood from anorexia. But who better to stage a fatal accident or natural death than a medical doctor?

A knock on my door interrupted my musings.

"Yes?" I called.

Mercy walked in and flipped on the light switch. Her zirconia tennis bracelet glittered in the glow of the overhead lamp. She gave no indication that anything was amiss.

"Time to check your vitals again," she said, and proceeded to do so.

"Your heart rate is a little high," she said. "Not surprising, given what you've just been through."

Oh no. Was she onto me?

"That stabbing was extremely disturbing, and especially for you, since you were the first to help that poor girl."

"Oh. Yeah, right."

"How are you feeling now?" she asked.

"Actually, not too good," I said. "I don't think I'll be able to fall asleep without my usual nightcap. Do you have anything I can take?" Of course I had no intention of doing any such thing, but I was keeping up my alcoholic appearance.

"Let's see how you do, and if you need some sedative medication later, we'll get it," Mercy said.

"Okay, I guess."

She left, and I mentally patted myself on the back. Mercy had found me right where I was supposed to be, and in an apparent state of withdrawal anxiety.

There wasn't anything more I could do that night. I was trapped in my room. Frustrating, but I had no choice.

I went into the bathroom to prepare for bed. The vanity was stocked with typical spa luxury amenities—triple-milled shea butter soap, jasmine mint whitening toothpaste, gum-massaging comfort grip toothbrush, and aromatherapy shampoo, conditioner, and lotion—all bearing The Oasis's logo, the name and a palm tree silhouette in aqua on a white circular background. Exactly the kind of stuff spa guests typically stuffed in their luggage and took home. They might not view that as stealing, but the spas sure did, building the costs of the losses into their rates. Not that rates were an issue for The Oasis's clientele.

The memory of Jessica's blood still soaked my mind, if not my body. I needed to wash it off. I spotted a bottle of bubble bath. I picked it up and read: "a rich exotic blend of lavender, bee blossom honey with white orchids, and warm, woody undertones of Indian amber delicately completed with a touch of Tahitian vanilla." Sounded like a damn wine.

I turned on the hot water in the tub, poured the bottle under the running faucet, stripped, and slid in. I released my long hair from its ponytail and shampooed it. When I emerged from the bath, I indulged in the body lotion, face cream, and toothpaste.

Nice. The textures and scents took me back to my Boca Babe days. Along with everything else, I'd left all that behind—I now used generic products from the Publix grocery. As I often do, I felt the tug to return to my former ways. Which is exactly why I didn't use those luxury goodies anymore. They were an enticement, ready to suck you back into that whole soulless lifestyle.

I left the bathroom and slid under the bed sheets. One-thousand-thread-count, I perceived immediately. Great. Another allure to relapse into self-indulgence. I slid back out, went back into the bathroom to put on a plush terry robe that hung there, then lay on top of the bed.

And laid there.

The bath had done nothing to remove the images of Jessica's spurting blood from my mind. What I'd told Mercy about not being able to sleep was coming back to bite me in the ass. Jeez, maybe I did need my nightly glass of Hennessy.

Nah. It was just the case keeping me up. If I needed anything, it was my Hog.

So there I remained in a state of agitated wakefulness, Mercy popping in to check my vital signs every four hours as I pretended to sleep. Damned if I'd take any drugs they might offer me. That could be deadly.

I finally drifted off just as dawn broke. I was startled awake by a much-too-cheerful "Good morning!"

I opened my eyes to a short, bespectacled, bald guy who introduced himself as Daniel, the nurse on the new shift. "How are we feeling?" he asked.

We? I didn't know feelings were collective. But since he apparently thought so, I said, "You tell me."

"I think we're feeling a little irritated, aren't we?"

A little?

"That's perfectly normal, Hailey," he went on. "But congratulations—you've just achieved your first night of sobriety."

"So what, am I going to get a medal?"

"Not just yet, but in another six days you will."

Seriously? *Okay, get a grip*, I thought. "So . . . what are *our* plans today?"

"I'll let you get dressed."

What, *we* weren't getting dressed?

"Then I'll escort you to breakfast, and then you're scheduled for a psych evaluation. After lunch, you'll attend a group educational session."

"Okay." I started to get up. "Wait. I don't have any fresh underwear. When I arrived here, I wasn't planning to spend the night."

"No problem. We have a boutique shop on site that has everything you need."

Oh, right. I'd forgotten about the gift shop that Mercy had told me about the day before.

"How about I take you there first, then you can come back and change before breakfast?"

"Sounds good."

He left the room, and I went to "void," as Mercy had termed it, and brush my teeth. When I emerged from the bathroom, I saw the still-rumpled bed and thought, *the help will take care of that.* Oh my God, I had really slipped back into the Boca Babe worldview. Like I said, those toiletry treats were treacherous.

I made the bed, pulled on my jeans and The Oasis polo shirt from the night before, and set off to raid the boutique on Gitta's dime.

THE SLEEK BOUTIQUE boasted minimalist décor in aqua and white, designed to showcase the objects of desire: Lilly Pulitzer resort wear, David Yurman jewelry, Judith Lieber handbags. One dependency The Oasis obviously wasn't treating—but rather, was feeding—was acquisition addiction.

Fighting the temptation to touch and admire the wares, I headed to the back, where a discreet, silver-framed sign indicated "Ladies Intimates." When I saw the intricate, lacy La Perla thongs and bras, my vajayjay perked up, reminding me that Lior was to arrive that night. *Hot damn!* I had to find out what the hell was going on in this place pronto, so that I could reunite with my man.

I snagged a matching set in black with red trim and charged the several hundred bucks to my—that is, my client's—account. Hey, it was a legit business expense.

The Boca Babe wannabe at the counter wrapped my purchase in tissue paper, placed it in paper bag (bearing The Oasis logo, natch), and walked around the counter to hand it to me. "Enjoy!" she chirped.

Daniel escorted me back to my room, where I changed, and then to the dining room. It was clear the staff wasn't going to leave me out of their sight for long. We passed a few patients along the way, but I had no opportunity to eavesdrop or interrogate.

The dining atrium buzzed with conversation. The same patients appeared to be at the same tables they had the night before—minus, of course, Jessica and Amber. The place was just like a high school lunch-room, with cliques staking out their territories. You had your jocks (the T'ai Chi masters), your cheerleaders (the water sprites), your stoners . . . except the latter covered everyone in here.

As before, Gitta waved frantically at me from her corner table. This time, Lars wasn't with her. I went to join her, striding through the room with an air of smug confidence. I was my own woman—part of no supercilious in-group. Besides, there's nothing like a new set of lingerie to make you walk tall and proud.

Along the way to the table, I caught snatches of conversation.

"I'm telling you, something bizarre is going on in here."

"Can you believe the way Amber stabbed Jessica right in the neck?"

"All that blood—I just about passed out. I've already talked to my lawyer. He's going to sue this place for infliction of extreme emotional suffering." Leave it to a Boca Babe to focus on her own distress rather than that of the real victim.

I reached Gitta's table. Today she was attired in a silk, flowered form-fitting dress with gold espadrilles. But, bereft of makeup and showing dark under-eye circles, she looked as though she hadn't gotten any more sleep than I had. She confirmed that when I sat down.

"Harr . . . uh, I mean, Hailey, I couldn't sleep all night," she whispered forcefully. "I keep thinking they're going to get me next. What are you doing about it?"

Oh, great, here we went again with her paranoia.

"Gitta, there's no rational reason to think you will be attacked," I whispered back with equal force. "All the victims have been teenagers. To restate the obvious, you are not. You haven't been for twenty years. Own it."

She gave me a glare but then said, "Kevin told me the same thing. Except much more nicely."

"Oh? When did you speak with him?"

"He came to visit me last night, to comfort me after . . . everything that happened."

"And did he tell you anything about the police investigation?

"No. He just repeated what Detective Snyder said yesterday—that Kevin can't work on the case because of his relationship with me."

"Okay," I said. "Well, I'm glad he was here to support you." I was even more glad that I hadn't crossed paths with him, which would have blown my cover.

Jason, the server, appeared, bearing a large chalkboard underneath his arm. "Ladies, I apologize for last night's disruption. And once again, I'm sorry, but the menus have gone missing. Here are this morning's choices." He propped the chalkboard onto an empty chair. In flowery script, it read:

Potato, Sausage, and Spinach Breakfast Casserole
Broiled Portabella Topped with Creamy Scrambled Eggs
Citrus salad with Mint Sugar
White Chocolate Raspberry Muffins
Brown Butter, Ginger, and Sour Cream Coffee Cake
Almond-Banana Smoothie

All that was missing was a Mimosa or a Bloody Mary. *Bloody hell.*
"Shall I bring coffee?" Jason asked.
"Yes!" Gitta and I said in unison.
"Regular or decaf?"
"Regular." In harmony again.

Jason departed, and out of the corner of my eye I saw the foursome at the table next to ours get up and leave. Jason returned with our coffee in a silver pot and poured it into china cups set on paper doilies atop saucers. He took our orders (casserole and coffee cake for me, smoothie for Gitta), then cleared the other table.

When he left, toting the chalkboard and tableware, two women approached. Glancing over, I saw they were Dr. Stillwater and Gardenia LaFleur, the dead teens' foster mother. Stillwater's pale yellow hair framed a matching pale face, while Gardenia's caramel complexion bore ashen undertones that belied the cheerfulness of her floral chinoiserie dress. Stillwater's hand lay on Gardenia's back as Gardenia wiped her eyes with a tissue.

As they sat at the next table, Stillwater smiled at us and said, "I hope you both got some rest last night."

We nodded and smiled back.

As Stillwater turned away to talk to Gardenia, Gitta started to say something to me. I gave her a kick under the table and shifted my eyes to the duo next to us. I wanted to hear what they had to say. To her credit, Gitta got the message, shutting up and drinking her coffee.

"I know what a terrible loss this is for you, Gardenia," I heard Stillwater say.

"Yes, they were all my kids—Demarcus, Angel, Kenyatta, Jessica, and Amber. Even though they weren't really mine, of course, but you get attached to each one. It's an occupational hazard."

"Of course. We doctors get attached to our patients, too, even though we strive to keep a professional distance. You can't help but be human."

"Yes," Gardenia sighed. "And this is taking a toll on my health. My blood pressure is sky high, and I've had to take more insulin shots for my diabetes."

"You need to take time for yourself," Stillwater said. "What kinds of activities do you find relaxing?"

"Oh, gardening. That's what my mother named me for, you see. I inherited her love of flowers. I can just lose myself in a garden."

"Then why don't you take some time to enjoy our beautiful grounds here?"

Jason arrived with our meals and with the chalkboard menu for Stillwater and Gardenia. Their conversation, and my attention, turned to food.

Stillwater remained my primary (okay, only) suspect, although I sure as hell didn't want to tell Gitta that with the doctor sitting right there. On the other hand, Stillwater seemed very empathetic to Gardenia. Could she really be so cold as to kill the kids and then comfort the bereaved survivor?

Did I have to ask? Of course—anyone could be a walking psychopath, a social charmer with an empty core.

As Gitta and I finished our meals, Daniel, the nurse, approached. "Hailey, it's time for your psych eval."

"Okay, I'll be right there." I hoped he'd leave so I could possibly do some snooping on my way to the psychologist's office. But no such luck.

"I'll wait for you outside the dining area so I can show you the way," he said.

"Are you going to be okay?" I asked Gitta.

"I guess so. I have an appointment for individual counseling soon."

"Okay then, I'll see you later."

I rose, nodded to Stillwater and Gardenia, and strode toward the atrium door, still feeling good in my new unmentionables. I might be closing in on forty, but right then it didn't look so bad. I still had my rockin' bod, thanks to my Krav Maga workouts. And I was looking forward to a workout of a different sort with my Krav Maga instructor.

About halfway to the door, I was intercepted by one of the water sprites. She was an ash blonde wearing a short Pucci dress. "Hey, you're new here, right?" she asked, her voice raspy.

"Uh-huh," I said.

"Want to score some dope?"

"Excuse me?"

"Whatever you want, I can get. Oxy, crack, smack, meth. Any form you want, too—swallow, smoke, snort, or shoot up. My name's Lisa. Everyone comes to me." Sounded like she had a flourishing drug trade going on in there.

"Uh, how much?" I asked, playing along.

She curled her lip. "What's the matter with you? Girls don't pay. Guys do. Just use your talents. You know, you service them, they pay me, and I get you what you need."

Oh. So she not only had a drug trade going but a prostitution ring as well. Operating her own little business-within-a-business. Quite the entrepreneur.

"Thanks for the offer," I said, "but I'll pass."

Her gaze swept over me from head to toe, and she curled her lip again.

I turned to go.

"Screw you, bitch!" she growled under her breath. "You're too old anyway!"

Chapter 11

TOO OLD? ME? In my hot new underthings? Who did this little pip-squeak think she was?

Oh yeah, she was a pimp. Why was I letting *her* get my goat? This place was definitely messing up my mind.

I left her and the dining atrium and followed Daniel to the office of Sanjay Singh, the psychologist who was to evaluate me. This was a pro-spect I did not relish. As far as I was concerned, psychology was a bunch of mumbo jumbo. Riding my Hog was the only therapy I needed.

Daniel ushered me into an anteroom. The door to the inner office was closed. "Please have a seat," he said. "Dr. Singh will be with you in a moment. I'll be right down the hall if you need anything."

"I'll be fine," I said, and he departed.

The room was furnished in The Oasis's signature Moorish style. I sat on a tasseled brocade ottoman before an inlaid-tile coffee table, which I was not surprised to see was barren of reading material. How-ever, a nice big flat-screen TV was mounted on the wall. Though it was off, it called out to me: *Sit! Relax! Vegetate while I fill your mind with vainglori-ous vapidity and create cravings for things you didn't know you needed.*

This was why I didn't have a TV at home. Marx had said that reli-gion was the opium of the masses. That was before the advent of the boob tube.

What the hell, I'd only be here a few minutes. I grabbed the remote, sat down, pressed the power button, and started channel surfing. After cycling through *Millionaire Matchmaker, Who Wants To Be a Millionaire,* and *Secret Millionaire,* I settled on the local news.

A helmet-haired, wrinkle-free, red-lipsticked female android (would that be a gynoid?) recited the current events.

A man had entered a McDonald's flashing a fake gun and a badge, claiming he was a cop and deserved free food. "The man was arrested for impersonating a law enforcement officer and improper exhibition of a firearm," the newscaster said.

Now, wait a minute. If it wasn't really a firearm, how could he improperly exhibit it?

Jeez, I was strategizing the guy's legal defense. *Whatever.* Not my problem. Where the hell was this Dr. Singh anyway?

"Next," said the newscaster, "we have some details for you about the arrest of a suspect in the murder of sixteen-year-old Demarcus Pritchett yesterday at The Oasis treatment center in Boca."

I sat up straight.

"According to a police spokesman, Jacques Bertrand, a Haitian national, was discovered with the victim's blood on his hands and clothing. Additionally, his fingerprints were found on the murder weapon. The police would not disclose a potential motive for the crime. Channel 17 had an exclusive interview with the suspect's wife late last night. She did not wish to be identified but did agree to speak with us."

The scene cut to a woman's face cast in dark shadow.

"My husband is innocent," she said in a thick Haitian Creole accent, her voice electronically altered. "He would not harm anyone!" she sobbed.

"Have you had a chance to speak with your husband since his arrest?" an off-camera male voice asked.

"Yes, I visit him in jail. He say he find stabbed boy in hedges in The Oasis. He try to help the boy, that is how he got blood on himself."

Hmmm. So the gardener had come upon Demarcus before Gitta and I had.

"Why didn't he call for help?" the reporter asked. Exactly my question.

"My husband afraid of police. In Haiti, police are torturers. He thought police would not believe him, so he try to run away." The woman broke down in sobs.

And of course, the man had been right—the police didn't believe him. But I wasn't convinced that the gardener was the killer. Hanging the blame on a frightened, poor-English-speaking suspect seemed awfully tidy and convenient. And the police weren't disclosing a motive—perhaps because they didn't have one? There was much more going on with the teens at The Oasis—and my Inner Vigilante wouldn't rest until I found out what it was.

I shifted on the ottoman.

"And now," the newscaster said, "a report from the statewide school principals' convention that is meeting this week at the Boca Beach Hilton."

Oh yeah, Enrique had said something about that.

"Our own River Sims is on the scene. River?"

The image changed to a male reporter standing in the hallway of the Hilton. People attired in suits, ties, and heels bustled past.

"Thank you, Lake," River said.

Jeez, who was next—Ocean?

River inclined his head to the camera. His hair didn't move. "Lake, the hot topic of discussion here this week is high-stakes standardized achievement testing. This is an acutely controversial subject among principals, teachers, parents, administrators, and legislators. The State Department of Education grades schools on their performance based largely on their students' test scores. Those schools that do well are rewarded with acclaim and monetary resources. Attendees here at this conference are asking: Are the tests biased? Do they place too much pressure on kids? And do they force teachers to 'teach to the test' rather than developing students' critical thinking and creative skills? Here to give us some perspective on this divisive issue is the president of the Florida Principals Association, Ocean Waverly."

But of course.

Where was Singh already? I was bored. Not having kids myself, and having successfully escaped high school, this was not a subject that held my interest. However, my alternatives—the various *Millionaire* shows—were no more appealing.

A blonde wearing a sea foam-colored suit and matching contact lenses appeared on the screen.

"Ms. Waverly," the reporter said, "what is the association's position on standardized testing?"

"I'm so glad you asked, River. The Florida Principals Association recognizes that testing is a complex issue fraught with high emotion. We realize that a test does not fully reflect a child's academic potential. At the same time, standardized tests provide us with measurable bench-marks to help kids succeed. The bottom line is, for me, it's all about my kids."

This woman should run for higher office. She had the art of talking while saying nothing down cold.

"But what about recent scandals from around the country where teachers, principals, and even a school board superintendent have been caught cheating—changing their students' test answers—in order to jack up their schools' ratings and increase their funding?" River asked.

"There will always be a few bad apples," Ocean said. "That doesn't mean the whole system is fatally flawed. In my school, my kids are paramount. And I know if you ask any other principal here, they'll tell you the same thing."

"All right, thank you for joining us, Ms. Waverly. Reporting from the Boca Beach Hilton, this is River Sims. Back to you, Lake."

"Thank you, River. Coming up, you won't believe what a local man found on the beach this morning. This is a story you won't want to miss, so don't go away, we'll be right back."

A commercial came on showing an elderly lady holding a hand to her head, looking befuddled. "Attention seniors!" a male voice boomed. "Is your memory slipping? Do you find yourself walking into a room and forgetting why you're there?"

The scene switched to the woman entering a kitchen, then looking around aimlessly. "Do you forget where you put your car keys? Or your car?" Cut to the woman gazing around a parking lot. "Have you lost your focus, your concentration?" said the male voice. "Now there's a revolutionary new cure—Turbo Brain."

A bottle of the stuff appeared on screen. "This proprietary nutritional supplement has been clinically proven to improve cognitive ability. And it's in liquid form, so there are no hard-to-swallow pills. Just two drops in a glass of water or juice will turbocharge your brain for hours. A twelve-ounce bottle is only $9.99—with a no-risk, money-back guarantee." The numbers flashed on the screen in bright red. "Turbo Brain is available now in your local drugstore, nutrition shop, or supermarket. Get yours today."

I pressed the mute button in disgust. As a Scam Buster, I knew a con when I saw one. These kinds of pitches for miracle "cures" for everything from arthritis to zinc deficiency were rampant in Boca, with its large senior population. Since they were billed as "nutritional supplements" rather than medications, the manufacturers could make any claim they wanted, with no regulatory oversight.

But that was hardly my problem right now. I tapped my foot in impatience. Dammit, I'd been in The Oasis nearly eighteen hours and didn't have any solid leads. And I needed to be out of there by this evening so I could reunite with Lior when he returned from Israel. I needed some strategy . . . maybe I could wring some info out of Singh.

However, he still hadn't shown up when the news came back on. I unmuted Lake.

"A South Florida resident made an unusual discovery this morning. You won't believe your eyes. But first. A thirty-two-year-old man has died after consuming dozens of roaches and worms in an eating contest at an exotic pet store in a quest to win a rare python. The cause of death is unknown pending autopsy results."

Seriously? The cause of death was unknown?

"And now. A blue eyeball the size of a softball washed up on the beach today. Take a look at this!"

The scene cut to the said object, draped in seaweed, rolling in the surf as a gaggle of near-naked beachgoers looked on with horrified expressions. "This was the scene early this morning on the Boca Raton beach," Lake said. "At this point in time, Florida Fish and Wildlife officials have placed the eyeball on ice and will analyze it to determine its source. They say it may be from a whale, a giant squid, or a large fish."

What, it wasn't from a Martian or from some mutant experiment at a rogue eye clinic?

As we say down here, only in Florida.

The door to the inner office swung open, revealing a tall, olive-skinned man dressed in a long scarlet robe with a flared skirt. A matching turban on his head nearly brushed the top of the door frame. A graying beard flowed from his chin to his chest. A six-inch dagger rested in a sheath at his side.

My self-defense instincts kicked in. I shifted in my seat, ready to jump up and kick butt.

"Ms. Holloway? I'm Dr. Singh," the man said in a sing-song voice. "My apologies for keeping you waiting. I see you've noticed my dagger."

Okay, so he was a perceptive psychologist.

"Not to worry," he said. "This is part of my traditional Sikh garb."

"Your garb is sick?" I leaned away from him. "Is it contagious?"

"S-i-k-h," he spelled. "An ancient religion of India."

"Oh, yes, of course." As if I knew that.

He didn't look fooled. "Won't you come in?"

I rose, clicked off the TV, and preceded him into his office. An ornate carved-wood desk with matching chairs upholstered in maroon velvet took up most of the space. Intricate Asian paintings of military battles and hunting scenes adorned the walls. We sat on opposite sides of the desk, which bore a computer monitor and a procession of hand-painted ceramic elephants.

"Let me share with you what we'll be doing here today," Singh said.

I nodded. Sure. Share all you want.

"My job is to administer some psychological tests to give us a better understanding of your personality so that we can tailor an individualized treatment plan for you."

Great—a personality probe. I would need to keep my Inner Vigilante under wraps.

"Okay." I smiled.

"We'll begin with a standardized test called the Minnesota Multiphasic Personality Inventory. I'll read you some true/false statements and enter your answers into the computer. Do you have any questions?"

"Standardized test? Is this anything like what kids take in school?" I felt myself freeze up, like those school kids who'd just been discussed on the news must have.

"Oh no, not at all," Singh sang. "There are no right or wrong answers here. Just give your honest opinion. Are you ready?"

I nodded. I was always ready to give an opinion, honest or not.

"It would be better if almost all laws were thrown away. True or false?"

True! Then my Inner Vigilante could be set free. "False," I said.

"I have often had to take orders from someone who did not know as much as I did. True or false?"

Hell, yes. My abusive husband. But I'd issued him the last order: "Go ahead, make my day!"

"False," I said.

"Much of the time, my head seems to hurt all over. True or false?"

False, but it soon would if this stupid questioning went on much longer. "True."

I needed to turn this interview around to my advantage. "Gee, Dr. Singh," I asked, "I guess this test could tell you if someone has a psychopathic personality. Have you ever run across anyone like that in here?"

"Interesting that you should ask," Singh said.

Yes! He was going to give up a clue.

"Do you feel that you might have psychopathic traits?" he asked.

Shit! He had turned it back around on me.

"No . . . just curious," I said.

"Let's continue, shall we?" he said.

So we did. After nearly an hour of questioning, I was ready to grab Singh's dagger and stab myself.

"Okay, Ms. Holloway, you've done wonderfully," he said at last.

"True," I said.

"Oh, no, that wasn't a statement."

"It sounded like one to me."

"Well, yes, it was a statement, but not from the test . . . do you need a break before we move on to the next test?"

Yeah, I needed a break—a break in the case. "I'm fine," I said, smiling. "So tell me, doctor, what is the most interesting or unusual interview you've had?"

"Ms. Holloway, this session is all about you, not anyone else. This is your time."

Right. And it was being wasted.

"Now I'm going to show you a series of cards with inkblots on them. Different people see different images in the inkblots. Just tell me the first thing that comes to your mind that you see in the card. Any questions?"

"Nope." *Just get this done and let me the hell out.*

He held up the first card, bearing a black and red splotch.

Blood. Spreading. On Bruce's chest. After I shot him.

"Ms. Holloway? What do you see?"

"Um . . . a butterfly."

He nodded, held up the next card. Black and red streaks.

Blood spatter. On my clothes.

"Uh," I swallowed. "Two people . . . playing a drum."

Next card.

Blood dripping from hands.

"Uh . . . a crab."

My faced burned. My skin itched. I couldn't breathe.

"Miss Holloway, are you all right?"

"Um . . . actually, could I use your restroom?"

"But of course. It's right out in the hall, on your right."

"Thanks," I muttered, and rushed to the door. In the hallway outside the waiting room, I saw the restroom sign. I pushed my way in, locking the door behind me. It was a single-user room with a toilet and sink.

I turned on the tap full force and splashed cold water on my face. I looked at myself in the mirror. My eyes were dilated, my hair seemed wilder than usual. I had to get out of here.

No. I would not run. I had a job to do. I had to bring those dead kids the justice they deserved. I had to stay.

I turned around and leaned against the sink. I closed my eyes, taking deep breaths to slow down my racing heart. My face was still warm, and my body broke out in a sweat. Was it unusually hot in there?

I opened my eyes and saw an air-conditioning vent in the ceiling above the toilet. I reached up a hand to feel for a breeze. There was only a weak flow. Then I saw something flapping inside the vent. Great—the airflow was blocked.

I climbed onto the toilet seat, one foot on either side. Bracing my-self against the wall with one hand, I reached toward the vent with the other. My fingers just managed to brush the grate of the vent and push it aside on top of an adjoining ceiling tile. A cascade of paper came crashing down on my head. My foot slipped and plopped into the toilet bowl.

Shit, shit, shit.

I extracted my foot and clambered to the floor, shaking off the water. My boot squished as I set my foot down. At least it was not the boot with my gun in it.

I looked down at the pile of papers, knelt, and began to paw through them. *What the hell?*

An instruction manual for a vacuum cleaner. A list of ingredients torn from a cereal box.

And menus. The missing menus from the dining room.

What was going on here?

One more thick sheaf had wedged behind the toilet. I grasped it and pulled it out, falling onto my butt. It was part of a phone book. The Yellow Pages. Starting in the R's. The other half of the torn phone book that Demarcus had been gripping when he was killed.

Chapter 12

I SAT THERE ON the floor of the restroom, holding the torn phone book, befuddled. What was this stash of printed material doing in the air-conditioning vent? Who had put it there? Why? I mean, I know all about bathroom reading, but c'mon.

The half of the phone book that Demarcus had clutched in his lifeless fist had ended in the R's, although I hadn't been able to get a closer look. Now, I saw that the first page of the section I held listed "Radio Stations." What, if anything, could that have to do with Demarcus's death?

Perhaps the phone book had already been torn before Demarcus got hold of it. But it seemed more likely that the tear was the result of a random split of the book as Demarcus and his killer pulled at it. But why would someone fight over a phone book? I guess the same reason Jessica and Amber had fought over the Coke bottle the previous night in the dining room—these people were addicts. Their actions weren't rational. They weren't in control of their emotions—they'd fight over anything.

And was the killer the same person who had stashed this half of the book in the ceiling? Probably. If you've fought to the death over something, presumably it's vital to you. And you couldn't just let it lie around in the open, since it would connect you to the crime.

So . . . whoever it was had to be tall and nimble enough to climb up there. The restroom was unisex, so that didn't narrow the suspect list by gender.

My thoughts were interrupted by a knock on the restroom door. "Ms. Holloway?" It was Singh. "Are you all right?"

Oh, hell. He expected me back to complete the psychological assessment. "I'll be right out," I called.

What to do with this pile of paper? It had to mean something. I didn't want to throw it in the wastebasket, but I couldn't just waltz out with it either. The only other option was to put it back and deal with it later. I gathered the papers and placed them on the toilet tank, then clambered back up onto the toilet seat and managed to stuff everything into the vent and replace the grate without another plunge into the bowl. When I stepped down, the water in my boot squished again.

I washed and dried my hands, then exited and went back down the hall to Singh's office, squishing all the way. The inner office door was open, and I found Singh at his desk, working on his computer. Probably writing up his diagnoses of my mental condition. That could make for interesting reading . . . but that wasn't what I was there for. Nor was I up for more of the inkblot bullshit.

"Dr. Singh, um, I'm not feeling very well," I said. "Can we finish this another time?"

"Why of course," he said. "What's the matter?"

"I . . . have a huge headache."

"That can certainly be a withdrawal symptom. Why don't I take you back to your room where the nurse can keep an eye on you? Then, let's finish our assessment another time soon."

"Oh, great." I shot him what I hoped was a wan smile.

We exited the office. He closed the door behind us and led me back to the detox unit. If he noticed me squishing, he didn't mention it. "Here we are," he said as he opened the detox unit door with his magnetic key card.

Daniel, the nurse, rose from his station as I entered. "How are we doing?" he asked.

"We have a headache," I said. "We would like to take a break out on the patio, if that's okay with us."

"Yes, by all means. There's nothing on your schedule until after lunch, when you will attend a psycho-educational group session."

Great, more fun times ahead.

"Would you like something for that headache?"

Yeah, a glass of Hennessy would be nice. Or a Hog ride.

"Thanks, but I think I just need some fresh air." I strode out onto the patio and sat on the edge of one of the green-and-white striped lounge chairs. The air held a hint of approaching autumn, meaning the humidity might have been eighty percent instead of ninety. Maybe my drenched boot would have a chance of drying out here.

As I pulled off my boot and sock, I noticed a ripple in the pond ahead. Then a pair of glistening eyeballs surfaced. Slick was back.

You are too funny, Miz H., he said in my head. *Just like Aunt Lana told me.*

What are you talking about? I demanded.

Your boot drying out? People *come here to dry out!* A plop of his tail sent up a spurt of scummy water.

At least one of us was amused.

When he saw I wasn't laughing, he knocked off his adolescent games.

What's up? he asked.

What's up in a restroom down the hall is somebody's secret stash of print materials. None of which makes any sense.

You're telling me, Slick said. *Who reads print these days? It's all cell phones and tablets.*

Whatever. I leaned forward in the lounger. *But that's the question—who? The what and the why are defined by the who. We—I mean I (jeez, I was starting to sound like the nurse)—need to find out who is behind this. But how? It's not like I can station myself 24/7 outside the restroom door. Even then I wouldn't know who's doing what inside.*

Eewww, Slick said, submerging his snout.

So . . . I need inside access, I mused.

Slick's ridged back rose above the waterline. *I hope you're not thinking what I'm thinking. Contrary to urban legend, we gators do not swim through sewage systems and pop up in people's toilets.*

Eewww, I said.

But you might have another friend who could help you out.

Well, spit it out, I said.

He squirted water through his savage teeth. Not the answer I was looking for.

If I had my cell phone, I could scroll through my contacts, but . . . okay, I'd have to do it old-school style . . . using my brain. I reviewed my mental list of friends alphabetically. A . . . nobody I could think of. B . . . Brigitta. She could no more monitor the restroom than I could. C . . . Chuck. I couldn't see how a gay, redneck, motorcycle mechanic would be a big help in this situation. D . . . blank. E . . .

Enrique! I said. *That's it! He's all about security technology; he's set up cameras throughout his hotel. I'm sure he could hide one in the restroom. It could transmit images to him remotely. Once someone climbs up to access the a/c vent, we will—in all likelihood—have our killer.*

You better not be pointing that camera at the can, Slick said. *That could land you a nice stay in the Big House. And a spot on the sex offenders registry.*

Gee, thanks for the words of wisdom. We'll aim it at the ceiling.

Well, hop to it, girl. He propelled himself to the opposite side of the pond and splayed out on the bank. Clearly, I was dismissed.

I needed to call Enrique from my room and somehow convey my needs without spelling them out, in case Big Brother was listening. Picking up my boot, I hobbled inside, one foot shod, the other bare.

Daniel manned the nurses' station.

"Would you happen to have a fresh pair of socks available?" I asked.

"Yes, of course. What happened?"

"Oh, my foot just slipped into the pond outside. No biggie."

Daniel reached into a drawer and pulled out several pairs of Tommy Hilfiger anklets in fuschia, sand, midnight blue, and other assorted shades.

"The plain black will do for me, thanks." He handed them over. "I'm going to lie down for a while," I said.

Once in the room, I picked up the landline phone and pressed the redial button, since Enrique was the last person—actually, the only person—I had called on that phone.

He picked up on the third ring. "Hailey, what do you need?"

What a true friend. He knew I would never call just to chitchat. It wasn't in my nature, and he accepted that.

"Enrique, being here in treatment is giving me such a new *perspective*. I wish I had a way to *record* my *views*."

"You . . . want a journal to . . . write your feelings in?" He sounded dubious. For good reason. He knew I wasn't the touchy-feely, poetry-writing type.

"Um . . . no, I just wish I could *capture* my recovery process from this *killer* addiction that had me in its grip . . ."

"*Ahhh* . . . like if you could have a video of what's happening there so you'd never forget."

"Yes!"

"That's wonderful, Hailey. I'm so glad to hear you're making progress in finding . . . yourself. I'd love to stop by later to see you."

"That would be awesome."

A knock came at the door. "Hailey, it's lunchtime."

"I gotta go," I said to Enrique. "I have a group session this afternoon. Could you make it around four?"

"See you then."

DANIEL ESCORTED me to the dining atrium and departed. As I was about to enter, I saw Gitta coming down the hall, hand in hand with a robust, rumpled, red-haired man—Detective Kevin Reilly. *Shit!* I couldn't let him see me—he'd blow my cover. And blow his stack.

I rushed into the atrium and slipped behind a large potted palm in the corner next to the door. Through the fronds, I peeped at Gitta and Reilly as they entered the threshold and paused. Gitta faced my way while Reilly faced her as they gazed into each other's eyes. I picked up a small pebble from the planter, set it on the floor, and kicked it. It rolled and lightly struck Gitta's sandaled foot.

Her gaze darted in my direction, her eyes widening when she saw me. The she raised her hands to the back of Reilly's head, stood on her tiptoes, and gave him a long kiss. When she broke it off, she said, "Thank you so much for coming to see me, Kevin. I feel so much better now. Talk to you tonight?" She batted her lashes.

"Of course. I'll call you, my love." And he left.

I emerged from my hiding spot. "Good save," I told Gitta. She had put her Boca Babe skills to good use.

Following a lunch devoid of murder and mayhem, Gitta went to a yoga session, and I was ushered into a small room where five other residents sat silently in cushy chairs facing a lectern. I took the remaining seat. I recognized the others from the previous night's trauma debriefing session, among them Kyle, the military vet with the leg prosthesis, and Renee, the woman whose young child had died. They all still looked pretty shaken, with wide eyes, unkempt hair, and chewed fingernails. Hell, I probably looked the same—or even worse.

I appraised them as potential suspects. Okay, the guy with the false leg probably would not have climbed up onto the toilet, but the others had no such impediment. That didn't narrow the list much.

The room's pale blue walls and the New Age tones emanating from an iPod in the corner did not appear to be exerting their intended soothing effect. In fact, the so-called music, with its shrill wind instruments accompanied by syrupy strings, rapidly got on my nerves.

I was about to get up and shut the damn thing off when Dr. Stillwater strode in. In contrast to the rest of us, there was nothing disheveled about her. Her navy blue suit was tailored to her figure, which was highlighted by a pair of sling-back stilettos that elevated her ass. A matching striped scarf was tied at her neck, giving her the appearance of a stewardess from the days when Pan Am ruled the skies. Her immaculate hair and nails furthered the illusion.

Could she be the one who'd hidden the stash in the ceiling? She was tall enough. But she could come and go as she pleased, unlike the patients. She wouldn't have to hide things on the premises—she could dispose of them in other ways.

"Good afternoon, everyone," she chirped. Far too brightly, in my not-so-humble opinion. "Today, we will discuss the psychobiology of addiction."

She stepped to the lectern and pressed a remote-control clicker. A white screen descended from the ceiling. With another click, a Power-Point projection popped up on the screen. Stillwater launched into a lecture, the gist of which was "This is your brain on drugs." Words like *mesolimbic system, dopamine,* and *synapses* were thrown around. I gathered that the bottom line was that substances, like drugs and food, and experiences, like sex and social interaction, that produced pleasure activated the brain's reward pathways and created cravings for more. In some individuals and with some drugs, the brain's function altered dramatically. Over time, tolerance built, requiring more stimulation to create the same effect, ultimately leading to a vicious downward spiral.

So in a sense, the kids in here had been hijacked by their own brains. But what had they been addicted to? Their medical records had indicated no evidence of drug metabolites in their bodies.

The way Stillwater was clicking through her slides with seeming glee made me wonder whether there was such a thing as PowerPoint addiction. After all, every press of the remote produced a gratifying click and brought a new image of a colorful brain scan. It was almost like a psychedelic show. It should have been accompanied by some Hendrix instead of that damn recorded harp.

"So what I want you all to take away from this," Stillwater wrapped up, "is that addiction is a disease like any other. It's not a moral failing. It's not a lack of willpower. And it's nothing to be ashamed of. It's a chronic illness like diabetes or heart disease. No one is ashamed of having those, and the same should be true of addiction."

Okay, sounded good to me. I slapped my knees and stood to go, ignoring the chatter that broke out among the other participants. Why was it that anytime a meeting of any sort ended, everyone started jabbering? Wasn't there anyone else like me who just wanted to escape to solitude? Besides, I needed to meet Enrique.

I slipped out of the room and down the corridors. For once, no staff member accompanied me. I finally had the opportunity to snoop—but not the time.

I reached the luxurious lobby.

Tiffani, the receptionist, looked up from her cell phone. "Ms.

Holloway! Where are you going?"

"Just outside to meet a visitor." I smiled.

She smiled back and resumed her phone fixation.

The air had warmed up some since I'd sat on the patio with Slick that morning. The royal palms undulated in the breeze, and a powder-blue sky embraced the grounds. Another perfect day in paradise. Not for those dead kids, though—they'd never again savor the joys of this earthly realm.

I sat on the bench at the edge of the broad expanse of verdant lawn. Just as I did, a sprinkler came on, splashing me with its spray. Was the damn thing rigged? I leapt off the bench and sprinted onto the driveway. Looking toward the security gate, I saw Enrique's big dark Beemer pull in.

He parked and emerged, took off his sunglasses, and scanned his surroundings, as was his habit. Spotting me, he ambled over, sidestepping the sprinkler to avoid any droplet on his pinstriped Armani suit. He had a distinct, languid stride that exuded self-assurance and sensuality.

"Hey, girlfriend," he said when he reached me, kissing me on the cheek.

"Hey yourself. Um . . . let's take a walk." We trekked along the drive to the side of the building, where the huge stone fountain burbled. We sat along its edge. I felt the cool mist of the water along the back of my neck. Suddenly, my mind flashed to another place, another time.

ROME. WITH BRUCE. We're sitting on another fountain, this one at the base of the Spanish Steps. Our tanned legs stretch before us. The sun glints off Bruce's four-hundred-dollar-a-cut blond hair.

We've spent the afternoon shopping along the Via Condotti. Bruce has bought me a Bulgari sapphire necklace and a Prada bag. We've gotten pistachio gelatos from a street cart and have sat on the fountain's edge to eat them and people-watch.

Bruce finishes his cone and reaches for the jeweler's hinged box. "Let me put this on you," he says. "I want you to show it off as we walk back to the hotel."

I smile at him. I know when we get to our room, everything but the necklace will come off, and we'll have a great session in bed. Spending fuels our sex life.

"Sure, honey," I say. "Just let me finish this ice cream first."

A look of irritation crosses his face. Shit. I've screwed up. I know better, but I've failed. When he wants something, I need to comply immediately. I gulp down the rest of the gelato. It's lost all its delicious nut flavor and silky texture, just slides down my throat in a cold clump.

I smile again. "Okay, ready."

I turn my back slightly to him. He drapes the jewels around my neck, his cold fin-

gers giving me goose bumps.

"Jesus, I can't get this clasp closed," he snarls. "What's the matter with you? Why don't you move your hair out of the way?"

Before I can do that, he grabs my hair and yanks it aside. My neck torques, and I feel a muscle tear. Tears sting my eyes.

"Okay, fine," he says. "It's done. Let me see." He puts a hand under my chin and pulls my face back toward him. "Are you crying? Are you serious? I just dropped ten grand on you, bitch."

He snatches the necklace and tears it off. One lone sapphire flies into the fountain. Bruce stands, shoves the broken strand into his pocket, and walks away, leaving me sitting, my tears mixing with the fountain's gentle spray of water.

"Harriet? Harriet!"

"Huh?" I blinked and saw Enrique sitting beside me.

"Are you okay?" he asked.

"What? Oh. Yeah, I'm fine. Thanks. Sorry."

"You sure?"

"Yeah, yeah." *Dammit.* I had work to do here. I had no time for reliving that old bullshit. That little reminiscence had spurred my Inner Vigilante.

Enrique reached out to hold my hand. Jeez, did I look that shook up?

Wait. There was something hard between his hand and mine. Enrique removed his hand, and I glanced at the object. A black plastic box the size of a cell phone, with a small glass lens on one end and a suction cup on the side. The video camera.

"Where did you want to put this?" Enrique asked.

"In a restroom."

"You're going to record people using the facilities?" His face scrunched up.

"Of course not. There's a bizarre stash of papers in the ceiling, and I'm hoping whoever put it there will climb up to access it. I want to catch them on camera when they do."

"Aha. Does this restroom have stalls?"

"No, it's just for one person."

"Okay, cool. Press this onto the back of the toilet, with the lens pointing up. Then push that button on the side."

I felt the button and nodded.

"There's an air card built in so it doesn't need to connect to Wi-Fi. It'll run for twenty-four hours before the battery needs recharging. The images will be streamed to me. I'll keep an eye on my monitor at the office."

"What if you're out of the office?"

"It'll save to my hard drive, so I can view it later. If I see something happen, I'll give you a call."

"Okay. You'll have to call my room, since I don't have my cell here. If I'm not in, leave a voice mail."

"Right. Code word: Social Climber."

"Perfect. That won't raise any eyebrows if anyone's listening in."

"This is Boca," we both said in unison.

We said our good-byes, and Enrique ambled away. His sultry stride reminded me of another man . . . Lior.

Lior! He was due to arrive at the airport in a couple hours. Dammit, I was supposed to have this case wrapped up so that I could pick him up. But the case was still wide open. I couldn't abandon my search for justice in favor of lust. But wait . . . why did I have to choose? If I couldn't go to Lior, he could come to me.

"Enrique!" I called out. He turned around, and I trotted over to him and explained my dilemma.

A broad grin spread across his face. "So you want me to deliver your lover boy for a clandestine rendezvous."

I shifted my gaze from his. I hadn't actually spelled it out that way. "Uh, yeah. I know this probably goes above and beyond the call of friendship, but . . ." I looked at the ground and kicked my toe into the grass. I mean, how embarrassing was this?

"Who are you calling a friend?" Enrique asked. "We're family, girl. Besides, you know I've been trying to talk you into getting some for years."

That was true. Much to my irritation, Enrique had never accepted my avowals of happily celibate widowhood.

"I'm going to be keeping an eye on the monitor for your . . . social climber," Enrique said. "But let me make some calls to the rest of the family."

"Not my mom!" I interjected. Although she'd be just as happy as Enrique to see me finally hook up. But please. It would be like being teenagers driven on a date by their parents, for God's sake. Enough to kill anyone's passion.

"Give me some credit," Enrique said. "Chuck may be able to pick him up. Or Leonard."

"Chuck!" Please. "Let it be Chuck." Having Leonard, my mother's lover, deliver my imminent lover was just too . . . gross.

"Okay, okay," Enrique said. "I'll text him now. Give me the flight info."

I did, and he relayed it. A few seconds later his phone pinged. He looked at the display. "Done deal. Chuck's on it," he said.

Now it was my turn to grin. "Now let's get this son-of-a-bitch murderer."

I MADE MY WAY back into the building and the bathroom where the bust was to go down.

I removed the camera from my back pocket, slid it behind the toilet tank, and pressed the suction cup against the porcelain. When I let go, the damn thing slid to the floor with a clatter.

Then the door handle rattled.

"Just a minute," I yelled.

Shit. I contortioned my body to retrieve the camera. I pulled it out and looked at the lens. Fortunately, it was intact. I'd read somewhere that moistening a suction cup would help make it adhere. I spit into the cup and pressed it to the tank again. This time, it stuck.

A loud knock shook the door. "Hey, hurry up," a voice called.

Evidently a Boca Babe who felt entitled to use any facility on demand.

"I said, just a minute!" I leaned over and peered behind the toilet tank. The camera was aimed correctly at the ceiling. I pressed the record button. Then, to project verisimilitude to the woman outside, I flushed the toilet, ran water in the sink and turned on the hand dryer.

Finally I opened the door to see Lisa standing there—the prostitution ringleader I'd encountered that morning. The one who'd called me old.

"Sorry, the air freshener ran out," I said.

Her eyes widened, and her lips curled back in disgust. She turned and stomped down the hall.

Damn, what if *she* was Social Climber? The camera would have caught her right then and there. Maybe I needed to rein in my snarky impulses when working a case. *Nah.*

I returned to my room to await Enrique's call or Lior's arrival, whichever came sooner.

I sat on my bed as dusk fell outside. The days were getting shorter in autumn, with twilight arriving around six.

Absent any external stimulation, my mind amused itself by imagining Lior's anticipated arrival. How he would look, how he would feel, what we would do. I was just reaching the part where he reached for my . . . when I heard a sound. Not the phone. The unmistakable rat-tat-tat of a Hog.

I sprang to the window. It was dark outside by then. I saw a single headlight approaching on the driveway. I made out the silhouette of a chopper with an extended front fork and elevated handlebars, straddled by two men. The driver boasted the beer belly of Chuck, the passenger—the hard body of Lior. At last!

I was out of my room in a heartbeat.

Daniel sat at the nurses' station.

"I'm going outside for a walk," I told him.

"No, you can't. It's almost dinnertime, and after that, it's Club Night, where residents have the opportunity to learn to socialize without the crutches of drugs and alcohol."

Right. I was planning to socialize in an entirely different manner.

"Sounds awesome," I said. "I wouldn't miss it. I'll just go out for a bit, then I'll go to dinner. I promise I'll be back in time for the party. Pretty please?" I flashed him a Boca Babe entreaty. That's when you tilt your head down, look up, and pout your lips.

I guess he was not immune. "Okay," he said. "But be back here in ninety minutes to go to the party. If you don't keep your word, we'll have to restrict your privileges."

"No worries," I said, and booked for the exit.

Once outside the building, I saw that Chuck had parked the bike and both men had dismounted and were removing their helmets. Lior wore a maroon V-necked sweater and black jeans. Chuck wore . . . well, who cared. It had been a couple months since I had seen Lior. He seemed taller, his shoulders broader, his biceps bigger. Odd. I mean, I should know his body after the years of Krav Maga training we had done together.

As his helmet came off, his black wavy hair tumbled out. He brushed it from his forehead, and his dark brown eyes rose to meet mine. Was it just reflected moonlight that glinted in his pupils? Suddenly I found myself standing next to him, not even aware I had traversed the distance.

"Hey," I said. Yeah, I know, real original.

He reached out and encircled my waist, fingers pressing into the small of my back, drawing me to him. He brushed his lips on the corner of my mouth. A day's growth of stubble prickled my skin.

"Hey," he whispered. The sound waves of his voice transmuted into a heat wave rolling through my body.

"Hey!" What the hell was that—an echo? No . . . it was Chuck.

"What about me?" he grinned. This time it *was* the moonlight, I decided, noticing how it shimmered the silver streaks in his goatee. Chuck spread his arms, and I put mine around his neck as he lifted me off my feet. "Ya okay here, kid?" he asked.

"You know I am," I said as he set me down. Chuck knew I could take care of myself. And that I'd learned to ask for help when I needed it. "Thanks for bringing him." I nodded toward Lior.

"My pleasure," Chuck said. "Great night for a ride."

"Aren't they all?" To a biker, there's no time you don't want to be out on the open road. Live to ride, ride to live.

"I'll leave you two, uh, to it, then," Chuck said.

"Thanks a lot, bro," Lior said, and they did that fist-knuckles-fingers thing that guys do.

Lior and I stood back as Chuck replaced his helmet, mounted his bike, and fired it up. The engine's roar rattled the ground as he took off.

I was alone with Lior . . . with no place to go. It wasn't like we could go to my room, with Daniel lurking there at the nurses' station. Wait . . . I had an idea.

"Come with me," I said, taking his hand. It felt as if we had never touched before. I was aware of every cell of my skin connecting with every cell of his.

I led him through the darkness around the side of the building. No one seemed to be outside. The foliage rustled, and the Intracoastal waters lapped the seawall at the far end of the property. Despite all the violence and craziness of the past couple days, at that moment The Oasis seemed very serene. We reached the Meditation Maze. The perfect place for privacy, with its seven-foot hedges and pathways illuminated only by the moon.

I unlatched the gate and led Lior down a few rows of hedges.

We turned a corner and came upon broken strands of yellow crime scene tape scattered on the grass, shattering the illusion of serenity.

Lior raised his eyebrows at me.

I whispered, "A boy was murdered here yesterday. And last night a girl was stabbed. I'm here on the case. Undercover. I'm sorry, but I can't leave here until I figure out—"

My words were cut off as Lior pulled me to him and brought his lips hard onto mine. The fingers of one hand curled in my hair as the other traveled down my spine. He pulled away, and his eyes looked into mine.

"Don't ever apologize for who you are," he said. His voice was soft but fierce. "Understand?"

Yes, I understood. I understood that this man loved me. He knew that seeking justice wasn't what I did, it was who I was. He knew my Inner Vigilante. Understood it, accepted it, embraced it.

It had been five years since I'd been with a man. I'd kept myself alone, isolated. Safe. But now the man was right, and the time was right.

I stroked his cheek and kissed him back, my tongue mingling with his, my body molding to his. I pulled up his sweater and ran my hands across his bare back, feeling the outline of every chiseled muscle. I licked the stubble along his jaw, savoring the sheer masculinity of him. I moved my hands to the front, tugging at his belt buckle.

He grasped my hands with his, pulling his head away. "Are you sure you want—"

This time I cut him off. "Yes. I want you. Here. Now."

"You have me. Here. Now. Always."

The leaves in the hedges rustled as we wrestled with each other's clothes. He pulled my shirt over my head, took a moment to eye the va-va-voom bra I'd acquired that morning at the gift shop. The moonlit glint in his eyes brightened.

He brought his mouth to my breast, his tongue teasing me through the lace, his hand moving to the back to unhook the closure. His fingers paused there.

"It's in the front," I said.

"Of course," he murmured. "Model number K253Z."

His hand moved between my breasts, and with a twist of his fingers, they were freed. He pulled me on top of him as he sat on the grass, my legs wrapped around his waist. I placed a hand on his chest, feeling the slow beat of his heart.

Slow? Exactly how excited was he? Okay, so he was a highly conditioned athlete.

Our lips met again as he lay back, pulling me with him.

The leaves rustled again as Lior quickly rolled us over, pinning me to the ground with his full, hard weight. My hand was still over his heart, and suddenly I felt it speed up, just as he cried out.

"Yes, baby," I said.

"No!"

He went rigid. I mean his whole body. "I . . . I've been stabbed," he gasped.

Then he passed out on top of me.

Chapter 13

"LIOR!" I SCREAMED. He was motionless, a dead weight atop me. Oh my god. Was he really dead?

No. My hand was crushed beneath his chest, and I felt his heartbeat racing.

With my other hand, I reached around his back, feeling for blood and a knife. There was neither. I pushed away with all my strength and rolled Lior onto his back. I shook his shoulders. No response. In the moonlight, I saw beads of perspiration forming on his face. I felt his forehead. It was burning.

What had happened? If he'd been stabbed, he'd be bleeding, maybe going into shock. Which would mean his heartbeat would be slow and weak, and his skin would be clammy to the touch . . . exactly the opposite of the symptoms he was showing.

I crouched in a Krav Maga stance, ready to fight, and looked around frantically. Where the hell was the attacker? I saw nothing but hedges reaching for the moon.

But at the base of the nearest hedge, something glinted in the moonlight. A hypodermic needle and syringe. Lior had been injected with something. He needed more help than I could provide.

"Help!" I yelled, quickly hooking my bra and pulling my shirt back on. "Somebody!"

Nothing. I thought of running to find someone, but I didn't want to leave Lior. The attacker might return. I screamed again, then heard the hedges rustling.

"Where are you?" a voice yelled. Was it a savior? The assailant? Or one and the same?

I didn't have time to figure that out right now. "Over here!"

I heard panting breaths, then Dr. Stillwater rounded the corner. "What's going on? Who is this? What happened?"

"His name's Lior Ben Yehuda," I said. This was not time for subterfuge. I pointed at the needle and syringe. "He's been injected with something. He's got a rapid heartbeat, and he's hot to the touch."

Stillwater knelt down beside us. "What did you inject him with? Heroin? Meth? I need to know!"

"I didn't! He was attacked!"

She whipped her stethoscope out of her jacket pocket and placed it on Lior's chest. After a few moments, she took out a penlight, opened Lior's eyelids one at a time, and flicked the beam across them. Then she took out her phone and tapped the screen.

My own heartbeat pounded in my ears. Through the pulsations, I heard Stillwater requesting an ambulance and the police and spouting medical terms. "Male, thirties, unresponsive, tachycardic, hyperthermic. Suspected stimulant overdose by IM injection."

Stillwater ended the call. "First responders are on their way. What was this man doing here? He's not a patient."

"He's a visitor. What are *you* doing here?" Hell, she could be the assailant.

"I was leaving work, heading to my car, when I heard you call for help."

Good story. But I couldn't trust her. Who was more likely to wield a deadly injection than a doctor? This attack had to be related to the others. Yet the method wasn't consistent. Demarcus and Jessica had been stabbed with commonplace sharp objects—hedge clippers and a fork. This was a different kind of weapon.

I could barely think straight. "Where is the goddamn ambulance?" I yelled.

As if in response, sirens wailed, then voices shouted.

"Over here!" I yelled.

At last, two paramedics rounded the corner with a gurney. It all seemed like a replay of finding Demarcus in that very maze the day before. The medics lifted Lior onto the stretcher, then started an IV in his arm and an oxygen flow to his nose.

"Take that syringe," I told them, pointing at it. "That's what he was injected with. The hospital might be able to analyze it to find out what it is. And it's crime scene evidence."

One of the medics picked it up with a gloved hand and dropped it into a plastic baggie. Then they wheeled Lior out of the maze as I hustled alongside, holding his hand.

Stillwater remained behind, texting someone on her phone. Probably Evans, the hefty CEO of The Oasis, who had run with her to the maze the previous day.

Just as the medics were pushing the gurney into the back of the ambulance, Lior's eyes fluttered open. They looked feverish in his flushed face.

"Lior," I said, squeezing his hand. "You'll be all right."

"I guess you really knocked me out, babe." A feeble grin appeared. I climbed into the ambulance beside him.

"What are you doing?" he murmured.

"Going to the hospital with you."

His grip on my hand tightened. "No. Stay here." He took a shaky breath. "Figure out who did this," he whispered, his words slurred.

"No, I need to be with you, to help you."

"The doctors . . . will give me . . . the medical help I need." Another labored inhalation. "The best way for you . . . to help me . . . is to find out . . . what happened to me . . . and to those kids."

His chocolate brown eyes held my gaze. Dammit, of course he was right. My Inner Vigilante wouldn't rest until it had the answers—and they wouldn't be found in the hospital. But I couldn't just leave Lior alone to the vagaries of the medical system. In his vulnerable condition, he needed an advocate with him.

But who? Of course—the Contessa. As a major donor to Boca hospitals, when the Contessa spoke, staff listened.

I ran a hand across Lior's forehead and brushed my lips to his. "I'll see you soon," I whispered. But his eyes had closed. He'd lost consciousness again.

"Please, miss," one of the paramedics said. "We need to go. We'll take good care of him."

"Where are you taking him?"

"East Boca Medical Center. He'll be in good hands there."

"Okay. Thank you." With reluctance, I clambered out of the ambulance. They slammed the doors shut behind me and sped off, the tires hurling gravel at my ankles.

Turning, I saw Stillwater standing there, framed in the moonlight. Her habitual mask of perfection looked frayed around the edges. She still held her phone in her hand. No doubt she had the Contessa's number stored in there, since the Contessa was a donor to The Oasis as well.

"I need to borrow your phone," I said. She opened her mouth to protest but apparently changed her mind upon seeing my expression. She handed over the device.

I scrolled through the contacts and found the Contessa.

"Good evening, Maria," she answered in her regal tones.

"It's me, uh . . ." I glanced at Stillwater and walked away from her. "Harriet Horowitz."

The Contessa, sharp as ever, didn't ask what I was doing on Stillwater's phone. Instead, she remained silent, waiting for me to convey the nature of my business.

"Lior has been assaulted. He's en route to East Boca hospital. Please make sure he gets the absolutely best care." My voice might have quavered just a bit.

"Certainly, Harriet. I will go there personally."

Damn, a tear slid down my cheek. "Thank you, your Highness."

I wiped my face, turned back to Stillwater, walked to her and handed her the phone. Only then did I see that the police had arrived. They were the same uniformed officers who'd been at the scene of Demarcus's murder the previous day—Hernandez and Fernandez. The hairy one and the bald one.

"Ms. . . . Holloway, is it?" Hairy—I mean Hernandez—asked.

I nodded.

"We'll need a statement from you."

We stood there as I gave him all the details. Well, not *all* the details. There was no need to know this had been a case of near-coitus interruptus.

Hernandez's face remained impassive as he listened and took notes.

"Search the area," he said to his partner when I was done. Then to me he said, "Do you mind if I search you?"

"What, you suspect *me*? What about *her*?" I pointed to Stillwater, who stood nearby, still texting.

Hernandez looked from me to Stillwater. Druggie vs. Doctor. Right. Who would a cop believe? If Stillwater was the guilty party, it wouldn't be the cops who'd find out—it was up to me. Sighing, I raised my arms and submitted to a pat down.

"All right, Ms. Holloway," the cop said. "You're free to go." He pressed the radio transmitter on his shoulder. "Fernandez, where are you?"

"I have no freaking idea," the voice came back. "This place is a god-damn maze."

I rolled my eyes. I wanted to search the maze myself, but I couldn't with the cops and Stillwater there. I stalked off and headed straight to my room, ignoring all the sundry staff along the way.

Daniel was still seated at the nurses' station in the detox unit. "How was our dinner?" he chirped.

"Um, just fine." I had no desire to disabuse him of his misapprehension about my whereabouts.

"Don't forget, Club Night starts shortly."

"Headache," I snapped through gritted teeth. "Going to bed."

"This is not an optional activity, Hailey," he sang to my retreating back.

I slammed the door behind me and plopped on the bed. My heartbeat still pounded in my ears. What was happening with Lior?

Okay, take a deep breath, I told myself. I could trust the Contessa. In fact, Lior would no doubt get better care under her watch than my own. My f-you attitude would likely get me booted right out of the hospital. Also, Leonard had already mobilized the "operatives," so the Contessa would know how to get a message to me once she had something to report on Lior's condition.

I looked at the phone. No red blinking light to indicate a message from Enrique. Damn—Social Climber hadn't shown up yet. Maybe because he or she had been the attacker in the maze?

A rap came at the door, followed by Daniel's voice. "Hailey? Time to go."

Okay. I wouldn't find out anything sitting in this damn room.

I opened the door. He eyed my attire—the same boots, black leggings, and The Oasis polo shirt that I'd worn all day.

"Is that what we would wear for an evening out?"

"We don't *go* out, okay?" Hell, I spent my evenings in the swamp with Lana.

"We have nothing more appropriate?"

Like what—a slutty, low-cut, high-hemmed number like I'd worn in my Boca Babe days? You could have bought a small car for the cost of those dresses, but that didn't make them any less cheap. "This is all I've got."

He smiled. "I see we'll have to work on appropriate attire. Not to worry, this is a common challenge among people with addiction problems. In the meantime, let's go ahead . . . and go . . . to Club Night."

Jeez, he sounded like some hyper TV host. *Let's go . . . Dancing with the Stars!*

We traveled along now-deserted hallways and entered a room jammed with people. Flashing multicolored lights bounced off glittering glassware and diamond earrings, necklaces, and bracelets. Beyoncé blared from the sound system as people gyrated on a dance floor.

What the hell? The place was a full-scale replica of a ritzy Boca night spot—complete with a wood-paneled, mirrored, fully stocked bar.

"Have fun," Daniel said and departed.

Okay. Hennessy at last. I headed for the bar and ordered a glass straight up.

The bartender was Jason, the waiter from the dining room, apparently doing double duty.

"I'm sorry," he said. "Perhaps you've misunderstood the purpose of this evening. It's to use coping skills to resist the urge to drink in this tempting environment."

My coping skills in this environment consisted of Krav Maga. I considered lunging across the bar and dispatching with Jason to get at the booze.

"What can I get you instead?" Jason asked. "Fresh-squeezed pomegranate juice? How about a passionberry smoothie with a hint of mint?"

"Water," I snapped.

"Excellent choice. Sparkling or still?"

"Wet will do."

"Irritability is a perfectly expected response in this situation. How about reciting a mantra to calm you down?"

"Okay. Hmmm . . . my mantra is . . . dry throat. Dry throat. Dry throat."

The kid gave up on his pep talk, reached under the counter, and procured a bottle of Perrier.

"Hold the lime," I said, anticipating his next move. "Just hand over the bottle, nice and slow."

He did so. I unscrewed the top and gulped the water in one swallow, then banged the bottle down on the bar.

"Make it a double?" he asked.

Jesus. "No."

I turned and looked around the room. In addition to the dancers, other patients sat or stood in clusters. I spotted Gitta, wearing a black Versace dress with gold trim, at a far table with a few of the T'ai Chi masters and water sprites. I walked over.

"Harr . . . Hailey!" Gitta exclaimed. "Please join us." She pulled out a chair, a trio of gold bracelets sliding down her arm.

Both the men and the women sized me up—the men as a potential plaything and the women as potential competition. Could none of them sense the pheromones coming off me from my recent encounter with Lior? The vibes that said my sexual interest in these guys was in the subzero range? My only interest in these people was as potential suspects—or leads.

I sat down. "God, isn't it horrible what's happened to those poor kids here?" I burst out. "First that boy in the Meditation Maze getting killed, then that little girl who was stabbed last night in the dining room. I am so freaked out . . . what do you all think is going on?"

If the staff had thought that the residents would have difficulty socializing without an alcoholic lubricant, they'd been mistaken. Murder and violence provided plenty of fodder of discussion. Theories about the deaths of the teens abounded. Someone on the staff was a secret agent of the foster care system and was knocking off the kids to save the state money. The kids were police informants, and the Mob had done them in. The victims had been abducted by aliens in the middle of the night, then killed to keep quiet.

Jeez, everyone was a damn detective. And a conspiracy nut.

But all I could think about was Lior lying in a hospital bed, struggling for life.

At ten, the club shut down. So much for the dose of reality. We were escorted back to our units like truculent teenagers.

Mercy, the nurse from the prior day, was back on duty at her station. This time her fake designer scrubs bore Missoni zig-zag stripes.

There was still no message from Enrique on my phone when I entered my room. I paced around the cage in frustration. There was no way I could sleep, not knowing what was happening to Lior at the hospital. I had to keep digging for the motive behind the attacks on the kids—and now, Lior.

I'd already discovered some common threads among the kids. For one thing, they were all foster children. For another, none of them had drugs in their systems upon admission. But I couldn't put together the information I had into anything meaningful. There had to be something else that bound the kids, and I kept thinking I might find the missing tie in those medical records.

My computer search of those records the previous night had been cut short by the appearance of the cleaning lady. Then the pop-up ad for the *National Inquisitor* had led me in a different direction. I needed to finish my records search.

I peeked out my door and waited until Mercy disappeared into the restroom. Then I quickly went into my own bathroom and grabbed one of the plush paper hand towelettes embossed with The Oasis's logo. I exited my room and slipped out of the unit using Enrique's magnetic key. I wedged the towelette between the door and the frame to leave it open a crack. I wasn't going to get stuck outside the unit again, like I had the night before. Then, again using the key, I entered the nearest office, Dr. Stillwater's.

I ensconced myself in the fiendish massage chair after ensuring it was turned off. I logged on to the computer with the same username— Green—and password—Bobcats98—as before, and accessed the master spreadsheet that contained all the patients' records. Previously, I'd been looking for medical information, like the nature of their addictions and their psychological assessments, that might provide some clues about the victims. This time, I needed to broaden the search for other possible commonalities among them.

I selected the four victims out of the patient list. First, Demarcus Pritchett. Then, Angel Romero, the boy who had supposedly died of a seizure. Next, Kenyatta Underwood, who'd reportedly succumbed to anorexia. Finally, Jessica Jarrett, who'd been stabbed with a fork in the dining room the night before. I systematically began looking through all the data fields, starting with name, date of birth, and so on. Nothing unusual . . . until I got to their addresses.

They were all different. Wait, I thought all those kids had lived in Gardenia LaFleur's foster home before they'd come to The Oasis. After all, she had called them her "children." What was up with that?

Now wasn't the time to stop and think about it—I had to gather as much information as possible. I kept scrolling across the spreadsheet. Still nothing interesting. Then I got to their school—they all attended the same one: Sterling Heights Academy.

I'd never heard of it, but it was one of those bizarre Boca misnomers. The only height in Boca was atop the downtown movie theater, which had reserved balcony seating, served cocktails, and had a dome to rival St. Peter's in Rome. Geographically, South Florida was as flat as the proverbial pancake. But "Sterling Heights" had the ring of an expensive private school. How would a group of foster kids have gotten into a place like that? And were there more kids from that school in The Oasis? If so, one of them might be the killer—or they could all be potential future victims.

I changed my search parameters to look for "Sterling Heights" in the "School" data field for all the adolescents in the facility. Only one more record popped up—Amber Moss. Amber—the girl who had stabbed Jessica. Had *she* killed Demarcus—and perhaps the others? I couldn't make any sense of it, but I had to get back to my room before

Mercy realized I was missing.

I logged off, crossed to the office door, and peeked out. The hallway was empty. I stepped to the door of the detox unit and peered through the crack I'd left open. Mercy was back at her station. *Damn.* I'd have to wait until she took off again in order to sneak back in.

It could be hours before she felt the call of nature. But . . . she couldn't wait that long to smoke. Craving would soon strike, as Stillwater had lectured the patients that afternoon. Sure enough, Mercy soon rose and wandered out to the patio. I saw the flicker of a lighter flame in the dark, followed by the bright red glow of a cigarette tip.

I opened the unit door, retrieved my towelette, closed the door behind me, and skedaddled to my room.

The first thing I did was look at the phone. No blinking red light, meaning no message from Enrique. Or anyone else, for that matter. Dammit, why had no one yet climbed up to retrieve the reading stash hidden in the restroom ceiling? And why hadn't the Contessa called to update me on Lior's condition?

My mind buzzed. I needed to talk the case over with someone. Leaving that confining coop, I went out to the patio.

Mercy turned to me. "How are you doing, Hailey?" she asked, exhaling a column of smoke upward above my head. How considerate.

"A little restless. Thought I'd come out and get some fresh air." *Cough, cough.* She was hardly the one I wanted to talk to.

Mercifully, she took the hint. "That's a wonderful idea. I'll leave you to enjoy the peace out here." She took one last drag, then tossed the butt into the pond.

A pair of jaws burst out of the water and snapped at her. She let out a yelp and rushed inside.

Yes! Slick was defending his environment from pollution by the likes of her. She might think twice before doing that again.

Anyway, he was the one I wanted to talk with in the first place. I sat down on a lounge chair.

Aunt Lana wants to know when you're coming home, girl, he said.

Awww.

As soon as you help me solve this case, I said.

Well, give it up, girl! What's happening?

I brought him up to date, ending with my discovery that the kids didn't live in the same home but did attend the same school.

I have no idea what that means, Slick pronounced.

Well, you're a big help, I said.

He swished his tail, propelling himself a few feet across the pond, then lurked there, instead of where he'd lurked before. Why did they do that? Maybe it was like humans rolling over in bed. You just had to find a more comfortable spot, even at rest.

I keep thinking about the National Inquisitor *pics,* he said. *You know, how maybe the victims leaked the snaps of Cody Keys and Jordan Mitchell being patients here, and how maybe that got them killed to stop them from doing it again?*

Yes, of course I know, I said. *Do you have any fresh ideas about that?* Okay, a hint of sarcasm might have crept into my tone.

Well, thank you for asking. As a matter of fact, I do. Who were you speaking with on the phone a short while ago?

God, he was just like Lana, always answering questions with more questions instead of just being straight up.

I thought back over the evening's events. *The Contessa.* I'd spoken with the Contessa about making sure Lior got the best care in the hospital.

Slick dipped his head under the waterline. Was that supposed to be a nod?

What does the Contessa have to do with the National Inquisitor? I asked.

Who founded the Inquisitor? Slick looked like he was trying to arch a non-existent eyebrow.

Hmmm. *Jimmy "The Spade" Spadola.* The guy had founded the tabloid right here in Boca back in the fifties, making a killing off its lurid headlines.

But he died decades ago, I said. *What's he got to do with anything now? Hellooo? This is Boca!*

Oh, yeah. Every rich dead guy leaves a young widow. Theresa Spadola was alive and well and a prominent Palm Beach socialite.

"So Theresa and the Contessa have to run in the same circles," I exclaimed aloud, bolting upright. "I bet the Contessa could convince her to pressure the *Inquisitor* staff to reveal the source of the leak."

At that moment, an unmistakable, imperious voice rang out from behind me. "Did I just hear my name?" The Contessa, a seemingly ageless woman, stood in the patio entryway in her equally ageless pink Chanel suit, dripping pearls and attitude. One arm clutched Coco, her short-haired Chihuahua, who was decked out in a matching pink Chanel ribbon, pearl collar, and pink nail polish. Hey, this is Boca—even the dogs accessorize.

The Contessa stepped out onto the patio. Coco was a perfect bite-sized snack for an alligator. Before I could issue a warning, Coco yelped, and Slick sprang from the mire a couple feet away, snapping his jaws in the air.

"Order!" the Contessa commanded.

Coco wilted like day-old lettuce, and Slick retreated into the pond's murky depths.

Damn, that woman had power. But what was she doing here? A sudden stab of fear ran through me. Lior. She'd come to deliver bad news.

She must have seen the blood drain from my face. "Sit!" she said.

I sat.

She took the lounge opposite me. "Your young man will be all right," she said. "I spoke to the doctors personally. He'll remain under observation for eighteen to twenty-four hours, but he is expected to make a full recovery."

My shoulders collapsed, and I buried my head in my hands. "Thank you, your Highness," I mumbled.

I took some deep breaths, then sat back up.

The Contessa remained seated, her spine upright in perfect posture, Coco alert at her side, ears perked and twitching. In times of hardship, some friends talk to you, some hold your hand, some pray for you. And some share silence with you.

"What did the doctors say?" I finally asked.

"It seems that Lior was injected with some kind of stimulant drug."

"Like what?"

"They don't know—it's not a common one like amphetamine or cocaine, they said. Whatever it was, it was a massive dose. The doctors said it was Lior's substantial muscle mass that saved him. A smaller person would have been killed."

A smaller person . . . *like me*.

Lior and I had been rolling in the grass. I was on top, then suddenly he was, just as the needle came down. "Contessa . . . I think *I* was the target."

She nodded. "Indeed."

Someone had tried to kill me.

Chapter 14

I HAD TO BE getting close, since someone had tried to do me in.

"I trust you will hunt down the . . . perpetrator," the Contessa said, her voice as cool and smooth as steel. She knew better than to try to talk me into leaving for my safety.

A shadow came over us as a cloud passed in front of the moon.

"I've arranged for Lior to stay in the hospital's Presidential Suite," the Contessa said. "And I've posted private security at the door. So you need not fear for him. You can devote your full attention to finding out who did this and what is happening here to my children." The Contessa, herself child-free, habitually viewed the beneficiaries of her largesse as family.

"Now, why were you speaking of me to that . . . savage beast?" she asked.

"I wasn't speaking to Coco," I said.

The Contessa rolled her eyes and inclined her head toward the pond. Oh, she was referring to Slick.

"Your Highness, I was saying to . . . well, I was saying that perhaps you could be of help on another aspect of the case."

"Of course I'll help," she said briskly. "What is it?"

I told her about the leaked photos of teenage celeb patients to the *Inquisitor*. "Maybe the deceased victims were the ones who snapped the pics with a banned cell phone and sent them to the tabloid," I said. "I've discovered that Dr. Stillwater had been viewing the *Inquisitor* website on her computer, so she knew about the leaks. You know how much this place values privacy and discretion for the rich and famous. What if Stillwater—or a henchman—killed the kids to silence them and scare off anyone else who got the same idea? And with Lior being stabbed with a needle and syringe—I mean, it practically screams 'doctor', right?"

The Contessa nodded with a sigh. "Indeed, no one is above suspicion."

"If we can find out who sent the photos to the *Inquisitor* . . ."

"Consider it done," the Contessa cut me off. "I will speak with

Theresa Spadola." She rose. "I shall be in touch." She departed, leaving a whiff of Chanel No. 19 and a few stray tan Chihuahua hairs in her wake.

I stayed outside for a few moments, trying to get a grip. My emotions were a mess. On the one hand, I was relieved that Lior would be okay. On the other, I was rattled that someone had tried to kill me—and might well try again.

As I rose to go inside, I realized, too late, that I should have asked the Contessa about all the kids being students at Sterling Heights Academy.

I SPENT A SLEEPLESS night on hyper-alert to any noise that might indicate the killer coming for me—and waiting in vain for a phone call from Enrique about Social Climber. And trying to figure out what the hell the hidden reading stash could have to do with the photo leaks.

In the morning, I joined Gitta for breakfast. Upon seeing me, she said, "Honey, you need some under-eye concealer." She whipped some out of her purse and offered it to me.

I restrained myself from slapping her hand away. "Uh . . . no thanks."

After we ordered duck confit Benedict and cinnamon-brown sugar brioche French toast from Jason, Gitta said, "Harriet, I spoke with Kevin last night. He's so steady and dependable. He calls when he says he will. It was never like that with my two late husbands."

"That's great, Gitta," I said. "I'm glad for you." And I meant it. Gitta had been used by rich, powerful men all her life—she deserved better.

"And you know what else?" Gitta went on. "I'm not as worried about myself anymore. I understand now what you said about me not being a teenager and therefore not being in danger here."

Wow. Progress.

"I think I'm getting close to finding the killer," I said. "So you just keep focusing on your recovery." Of course, I did not clue her in on why I thought I was getting close—because someone had tried to kill me. That would propel her right back into panic mode.

After the meal, Gitta went to get a hot stone massage and Dead Sea salt body scrub, while Daniel, who was back on the day shift, ushered me to the small classroom for another educational lecture. "Today you're going to learn about conditioning," he said.

"Hair conditioning?" I knew all about that from my former life, when I'd spent hours in salons undergoing hot-oil scalp treatments.

"No, a different kind."

"Physical conditioning?" I knew about that, too, from my new life as a Krav Maga mistress.

"I'll let Dr. Stillwater explain," Daniel said. "Here we are." He left me at the open doorway.

A few of the water sprites and surfer dudes were gathered in the room. Stillwater strode in on her high heels with her trademark self-assurance, wearing a gold-toned sleeveless dress that matched her hair. Seeing me, she strolled over, sat down, and laid a hand on my knee. I recoiled at her touch.

"How are you doing, Hailey?" she asked, gazing at me intently with her golden eyes—the eyes of a killer?

"I'm okay."

"The visitor log shows the Contessa von Phul came to see you last night."

"Yeah, we're, uh, old acquaintances. She's who I called on your phone last night."

"Yes, I saw that on my phone log."

"She came to tell me Lior's going to be okay, so now I'm okay, too. Thanks for asking." I watched her for a reaction to the news, but she maintained her placid smile.

"Yes, I already called the hospital myself this morning," she said. "I'm extremely relieved."

Sure she was. Relieved that she hadn't killed the wrong person. That could get messy.

"And don't worry, the police are investigating," she said.

Yeah, that made me feel a whole lot better.

"All right, then," Stillwater said. "If you need to talk, I'm here."

Right. As if.

She rose and proceeded to the front of the room. "Folks, today we're going to debrief last night's club experience."

Seriously? Did she expect the group to dissect and deconstruct who had flirted with whom, who had backstabbed whom, who was the best—and worst—dressed, and all the other morning-after bullshit?

"How did you all feel in the club?" she asked.

Oh, please. Discussing *f-ee-ee-lings?* That was even worse. Apparently, the others agreed with me, as they sat silent.

"Anxious, perhaps?" Stillwater prompted.

Heads bobbed. Then the chatter started.

"I felt out of place."

"I didn't know what to do with myself."

"It was torture."

"Man, I just wanted a shot."

"And a line."

Laughter broke out.

"Exactly," Stillwater said. "Do you know why you had these cravings?"

Yeah, I knew why I'd craved my Hennessy—because Lior had almost been killed, for God's sake. Maybe by this woman.

There was silence again.

"Because we're addicts?" one of the water sprites ventured.

"Skyler, you're not addicts," said Stillwater. "You are people with the disease of addiction. Your disease does not define who you are. But I have another point here. The reason you experienced cravings in the club is because of Pavlovian conditioning."

Okay, so this wasn't a bunch of addicts, it was a pack of dogs.

"I'm sure many of you took Intro to Psychology class in high school or college. So you remember that when Pavlov paired the sound of a bell with food, his dogs began to salivate merely at the sound of the bell."

I doubted this group could remember much of anything. But it did ring a bell for me.

"The bell is what we call a conditioned stimulus," Stillwater lectured. "It elicits a response due to its association with the unconditioned stimulus—the food in this case."

"So, you're saying if we put a dog in a club it will salivate?" a surfer dude asked.

Stillwater smiled. She may have been a murderer, but she evidently had far more patience with the dim bulbs of the world than I did. "No, Tyler, what I'm saying is, you all are conditioned to the pairing of alcohol or other drugs with a club environment. Whenever you've been in a club in the past, you've used and gotten high. Now you expect the same high when you enter a club. When that high doesn't come, you crave it. So we need to work on decoupling the conditioned and unconditioned stimuli."

She went on to talk about how it was necessary, early in recovery, to avoid the people and places that were associated with getting high, and to develop coping strategies for dealing with those situations when they arose later on.

"That is why we put you in that simulated environment last

night—so you could viscerally experience the dangers it poses to your sobriety, yet remain in a safe place here at The Oasis."

Yeah, right. Safe from a fake nightclub, maybe. But not safe from a real murder.

Chapter 15

ALL THE TALK of salivating dogs got my own mouth juices flowing, ready for lunch. I found myself anticipating a bell to ring, summoning us for chow. And I was not disappointed. Stillwater's phone chimed Pachelbel's Canon in D.

"That's our signal that this session is finished," she announced. "We'll break for our midday meal, then each of you has activities scheduled for this afternoon."

The pack filed out. I was in the lead, which I guess made me the alpha dog. My nose tracked savory scents of simmering sauces to the dining room. At the entrance, I found Gitta with her son, Lars, together with the Contessa and her actual dog, Coco, all waiting for me. The sight of the Contessa sent a stab of fear through me.

"Is Lior all right?" I asked her.

"Oh, yes, he is continuing to recover as expected. That is not why I'm here."

I let out my breath. Okay. He was going to be okay. That meant I would be, too. But I was still confused at the sight of her. Had she spent the night in this place?

Oh wait—her Chanel suit was a pastel blue this time instead of the prior night's pastel pink. Coco's ribbon had been swapped out to match. Gitta wore the same silk sheath she'd had on this morning, while Lars sported his Boca Country Day uniform of khakis, white button-down shirt, and navy blue blazer with insignia on the breast pocket. Apparently, he was on lunch break from his nearby school. He'd probably popped over in the family's Bentley.

There was no need for introductions, since Gitta and the Contessa were well-acquainted from their circles in Boca's high society.

Gitta grabbed my arm in her habitual frantic manner. "Her Highness has news for you," she whispered.

Already? Oh yeah, she *was* the Contessa.

Before we could speak further, Jason, the server, approached. "May I seat you ladies—and gentleman?" he asked with a nod to Lars.

We followed Jason to our usual table in the back, threading our way through clusters of seated patients. I spotted Lisa, the prostitute ring leader/drug dealer, at the table next to ours, attired in a low-cut Diane von Furstenberg wrap dress. She was in animated discussion with a handful of male and female patients. Must have been a business power lunch.

Jason handed us one menu to share. Jeez, why didn't they print up some more menus already? It wasn't like The Oasis was under a budget crunch. They could just charge the patients for the cost of the engraved, gilt-edged papers and leather covers.

As soon as Jason departed, I whispered to the Contessa, "You've found out who sent the photos of Cody Keys and Jordan Mitchell to the *Inquisitor?*"

"What?" said Gitta and Lars simultaneously.

I shushed them with a wave of my hand.

"Not entirely," the Contessa said, giving Coco a sip from her water glass. "According to Theresa Spadola's sources, the photos were e-mailed from an account bearing the username 'acquanaturale.' Does that mean anything to you?"

I thought for a moment. Something about it seemed familiar, but I couldn't place it just then. "I have no idea."

"I can do some hacking to find out who's behind that username," Lars piped up.

We all stared at him, including Coco, who took a momentary lapse from her laps.

"And . . . Jordan Mitchell is here?" he asked, sounding hopeful.

"No." Gitta and I said simultaneously. But each of us was responding to different things.

"Lars, you will not get enticed by that strumpet," Gitta said. "You are heading to MIT, remember?"

"And no, you will not do any hacking," I said. "As if you didn't know, that's illegal." Hey, it was one thing for me to conduct it, something else for me to condone it.

"Mom!" Lars dragged out the word to three syllables. He leaned back in his chair and folded his arms across his chest. I knew Lars was a good kid—an adult, really, in taking care of Gitta—but occasionally an adolescent peevishness seeped through.

"Your mother's right," I said.

"Miss Harriet is right," Gitta said at the same time.

Wow. Gitta and I were rarely on the same page. Either she really was recovering from addiction and *babeness*, or I was manifesting maternal instincts. Yikes.

"Is that the young lady who is a twerp?" the Contessa asked.

"The word is 'twerk', your Highness," Gitta said. "It's a . . . form of dance."

"Indeed," the Contessa sniffed.

"Hellooo?" I said. "Can we focus on the matter at hand?"

"Yeah, the case," Lars said, leaning forward on the table, apparently having come out of his funk.

"Actually, I meant lunch." So sue me, but I was still salivating. C'mon, admit it—you can't think when food is on your mind.

The four of us huddled around the menu. The Contesssa, Gitta, and I decided to split a bistro shrimp scampi pizza and pear-endive salad, while Lars, the health nut, went for the vegan Boca Burger on a twenty-grain bun with a side of quinoa-cashew mix and a glass of aloe juice. Jason took our orders and our menu, which he handed to the table next to ours.

"Well, thank you for getting that information, your Highness," I said. "I just wish I knew what it meant."

"Quite so," the Contessa said.

"There is another thing," I said, looking around to make sure no one was eavesdropping. The madam, her employees, and customers seemed to be engrossed in making a deal. I figured drugs and sex riveted them more than our conversation.

"I found out that the deceased adolescents—Demarcus, Angel, and Kenyatta—as well as Jessica, the girl who was stabbed, and Amber, the one who stabbed her—all attended the same school—Sterling Heights Academy."

"But of course," the Contessa said. "I could have told you that."

Sure, if I'd known to ask. I nearly snapped at her but bit my tongue.

That was the thing about an investigation—you couldn't seek something if you didn't know you needed to look for it. You couldn't sift the crucial from the trivial until it all came together in your head.

"So, what's the school connection?" I asked the Contessa.

"Well, you know I fund beds here at The Oasis for foster children. As you can imagine, many of them struggle academically. Sterling Heights is a charter school that provides individualized attention. Its specialized teaching approaches allow vulnerable children to succeed. In the mainstream public schools, they would fall through the cracks."

Jeez, she sounded like she'd memorized some promo brochure.

"I see," I said. So Sterling Heights was not a prep school for the privileged, as the name would suggest. Of course, Boca was king when it came to slapping on glittery labels.

"And in fact," the Contessa continued, as Coco, who had dozed off, snored in her lap, "Sterling Heights has worked miracles with these children. Since its new principal arrived two years ago, the students' standardized test scores have skyrocketed. The school has gone from an F to an A in the state's grading system."

"Yeah, but their lacrosse team sucks," Lars said.

"Young man, may I remind you that we should not speak ill of those less fortunate than ourselves," the Contessa said.

"Just sayin'," Lars mumbled. Then he went on, "It's like they don't even want to be out on the field. It seems like all they want to do is sit on the bench and read their textbooks."

Jason arrived with our order. Coco awoke, ears perked and nose sniffing the air. The Contessa picked shrimp off with a salad fork and gingerly fed them to her.

I, on the other hand, tore into the pizza like a rabid dog. Gitta ate the salad, while Lars, sullen again, bit into his Boca Burger.

Now that my calorie craving was satisfied, my mind was able to think again.

"You know," I said, "I'm following a couple leads here at The Oasis. This photo leak and . . . well, something else." They didn't need to know about the hidden reading stash. "But now that I know that these kids all went to the same school, I have to wonder if that is where the real motive behind these violent acts lies. What if I've been on the wrong track all along?"

Gitta, the Contessa, and Coco chewed that over in silence, but Lars sat straight up again.

"I can help you," he exclaimed.

I narrowed my eyes. "How?"

"I can go undercover in the school. I can observe what's going on, talk to the kids, hunt for clues."

Jeez. That was all I needed—a fanatical little PI apprentice. Save me.

"No!" Gitta and I said.

Coco jumped and proceeded to choke on a shrimp.

"Oh my god!" the Contessa screamed. "*Liebchen!*"

The madam and her group at the next table stopped their negotiations and stared. Jason rushed over, tore the beast from the Contessa's grasp as it gasped for breath, and squeezed it like a tube of toothpaste. The shrimp dislodged, flew in a graceful arc, and landed in the madam's cleavage. The woman screamed, and the pandemonium shifted from our table to theirs.

Jason handed the trembling Coco back to the Contessa. "Can I get you all anything else?" he asked.

We shook our heads.

"Awesome, dude," Lars said, bumping fists with him.

"I am most grateful, young man." The Contessa reached into her Chanel bag, pulled out a pair of Benjamins, and handed them to Jason, who smoothly slipped them into a pocket.

"Glad I could be of service," he said.

No doubt.

"So, as I was saying," Lars said after Jason departed.

"And as we were saying," I said, "no, we are not risking your safety by putting you in an environment where there may be danger." True, the deaths and the attacks had occurred at The Oasis, not at the school. But still, if the motive behind them was at the school, the place could well be perilous.

"So, what? Like you're going to go undercover there yourself?" Lars said. "No offense, Miss H., but I don't think you'd pass for sweet sixteen."

Great, kid. Thanks for the subtle reminder that my Big 4-0 was looming—tomorrow. And dammit, I had no good comeback to that one.

"C'mon, Mom, let me do it," he said.

"No, Lars. I couldn't stand to have anything happen to you."

"I can take care of myself," he said. "I've been taking care of *you* my whole life." He glared at her.

And she had no good comeback to that one. Neither did I. His statement was sad but true.

We all looked at the Contessa, the ultimate Boca arbiter.

"I am in accord with you, young man," she said at last, clutching the dog, who had once again nodded out following its near-death experience. "As much as I hate to think so, Harriet may be right that the source of these sinister acts is outside of The Oasis. And I believe you can be trusted to be both safe and discreet."

The kid beamed.

"I shall call the principal," the Contessa said. "You will begin classes this very afternoon."

Chapter 16

AFTER LUNCH, LARS and the Contessa took off to get him enrolled at Sterling Heights, intending to stop at a mall first so that Lars could swap out his preppy attire for something more befitting his new undercover persona, like a pair of low-riding baggy pants and droopy hoodie. Gitta headed down the hall to have some sinister-sounding brain-wave stimulation procedure.

I saw Daniel, the nurse, approach, and feared he was going to haul me off to the same thing. I braced myself for some Krav Maga action. I was ready to bust out of that lunatic asylum by whatever means necessary. But Daniel informed me that I was to attend an art therapy session in a half-hour.

"Can I just have a minute?" I asked.

"Sure," he said. "I'll wait outside the door for you. But no more than a minute. Punctuality is one of the lessons we need to learn here at The Oasis."

"Absolutely," I said.

I wanted to have a word with the prostitution ring leader, or, as I now thought of her, the Shrimp Pimp. The day before, she had made it loud and clear that I was too old for her enterprise. Seeing her again had gotten me wondering whether she had recruited any of the adolescents into her business. If so, what if the girls had refused to split their drug earnings with her? What if the boys had utilized the services but then refused to pay up? Could she have killed the kids over that? After all, prostitution and violence were inextricably linked.

I slid over to her table. She and her companions stopped talking and stared at me.

"Hey, I'm sorry about the flying shrimp," I said.

"That's okay, honey," she said. "I've had worse slide down my boobs, if you know what I'm saying."

Eeww. Jeez. Yuck. I felt like taking a shower right then and there to wash that image out of my mind and the creepy feeling off my body.

"Anyway," she continued, "I would have done anything myself to save that poor little dog. People? Forget about it. Most of 'em I wouldn't piss on if they were on fire." Or even if they weren't, I hoped.

"But dogs?" she said. "I'd lay down my life for them."

I guess everyone had a soft spot—gators being mine.

"Could we talk a minute in private?" I asked, nodding toward her lunch companions.

She looked me up and down. "You want to talk business? You haven't gotten any younger since yesterday, honey."

God, why these constant reminders of my upcoming fortieth?

"I know I'm too old to work for you," I said through gritted teeth, "but how about working *with* you?"

Apparently not one to bypass a professional networking opportunity, Shrimp Pimp turned to the rest of the table and said, "Scram."

Her companions left the dining room, and I took one of their vacated chairs.

"So, what'd you have in mind?" she asked.

"I see you've got a nice gig going in here. To tell you the truth, I've been in and out of all the rehab joints across the county in the last year. I know the staff in every one of them, and most of my friends are revolving through the doors, too. So it occurred to me, we could grow your business in these other markets. We could open up franchises. You get a cut, I get a cut, everyone's happy. What do you say?"

She pursed her lips. "I could go for that. As long as I retain majority share."

I paused as if considering her counteroffer. "Forty percent for me, sixty for you?"

"Thirty-seventy."

"You got a deal." I stuck out my hand.

She shook it, and I resisted the urge to wipe it. "Now," I said, "I think our most lucrative demographic on the supply side would be the eighteen and under."

"I feel you," Shrimp Pimp said.

Eeww. Again.

"I hope you can recruit them in the satellite locations," she said, "because this place is a bust."

"What do you mean?"

"The little rich bitches in here won't even talk to me. I don't blame them. They've got access to Daddy's money, so they don't need to sell their assets. What I don't get is, even those welfare kids turned me down. Both the girls *and* the guys."

"Oh yeah?"

"Yeah, you know what they told me?" She leaned forward, exposing more of her boobs. An orange blob of cocktail sauce remained stuck to her flesh.

"What?"

"They said they're not interested in sex. Can you believe that?" She raised her over-plucked eyebrows. "What teenage repository of hormones isn't interested in sex?"

I had to agree that sounded strange—although I didn't think sex and prostitution were the same thing. "Well, even if they weren't interested in sex, what about drugs?" I asked.

"Didn't seem to care about those, either. Weird, huh? If they don't care about drugs, why the hell are they in here?"

That was the million-dollar question.

BEFORE DANIEL escorted me to the art therapy session, I asked to stop in my room to brush my teeth. In reality, I wanted to see if there was a message from Enrique about the toilet cam. There wasn't. *Damn.* There was no point in calling him—I knew he would have called if there'd been any action. Frustrated, I exited the room, slamming the door behind me.

"Looks like we could use some relaxation," Daniel chimed from behind his nurses' station.

I glared at him.

"Finger painting should do the trick,"

"Finger . . . painting. That's a joke, right?"

"Not at all. Come with me."

I had a strong urge to flee. This had to be a new low in my PI career. The Oasis was turning out to be a sinkhole. But my work here wasn't done, so I had to tough it out.

Daniel led me to an art studio, a room with two glass walls that made the most of the natural light streaming in. Six would-be *artistes*, all of them adult patients I'd encountered before, sat around a circular table. Great. We'd probably come out of here with six variations on Edvard Munch's *The Scream*. Which was exactly what I felt like doing.

However, I was rendered soundless when none other than my old friend Lupe waltzed in, a red tiered skirt brushing her ankles and chandelier earrings brushing her shoulders beneath elaborately upswept hair.

Her eyes met mine in silent recognition as she proceeded to the front of the room.

"Good afternoon, everyone," she said. "As you all know, I am Dr. Guadalupe Domingo, the volunteer chaplain here at The Oasis. One of the spiritual services we offer is art therapy, which we'll be doing together this afternoon."

Figured. Lupe always was the New Age woo-woo type. She was a Mexican witch, for God's sake.

"Today, we're going to set our spirits free by expressing ourselves through art," she said. "One of the wonderful things about this process is that you don't need any so-called artistic talent. All you need is your fingers. Or your toes. Or any other body part you want to use."

Oh, God, no. Please . . . no butt prints.

"So we're going to make a mess, but a contained mess," Lupe said.

She reached inside a drawer and withdrew a plastic cover, which she spread atop the table. Then she pulled out some clear plastic ponchos. "Tyler, can you hand these out to everyone?" she said.

As Tyler did that, Lupe tore large pieces of butcher paper from a roll atop a counter. "Skyler, how about you place these in front of everyone?"

Finally, Lupe hauled out gallon buckets of paint in primary colors and set them in the center of the table.

"So," she said brightly, "just take your fingers, your toes, your hair, whatever, and dip it into the colors. Don't worry, these paints are non-toxic and will wash right off. Then apply the paints to your paper. Don't worry about doing it right or using the right technique. There is no right way or right technique. Just let yourselves go. Set aside your conscious thoughts and allow your subconscious to emerge. Your subliminal self will guide you in your expressions. Just follow it."

I loved Lupe, but this was bullshit. The only thing I needed to tap into my subconscious was my Hog. But maybe something meaningful to this case would emerge from the subconscious of the other participants. Yeah, I know, that was a stretch. Clearly, I was getting desperate.

Lupe put on some loopy music of flutes and pianos and lit a few aromatic candles. The group spent the next hour dipping into paints, then swirling, swaying, splotching, squiggling, and generally acting like toddlers in a playroom. And making the same kind of mess.

The resulting "art" was pretty much what you'd expect—the kind of masterpieces parents tack onto refrigerators. Except these were the Boca version. Instead of a little house with a picket fence, Skyler drew a faux Mediterranean McMansion with a backyard pool and lighted land-scaping. Instead of a stick-figure mom standing on a porch, Tyler painted a bejeweled Barbie-shaped woman provocatively posed before a Porsche.

When we were finished, everyone pulled off their ponchos and washed their hands in a sink in the corner of the room.

"My manicure is ruined!" one of the Boca Babes whined. Hmm. I wondered if her subconscious was equally beauty-conscious.

After we returned to the table, Lupe asked, "Would anyone care to share how they felt during the process?"

A litany of expressed emotions poured out, spanning the spectrum from "free" to "liberated."

"And you, Harr . . . Hailey?" Lupe asked me.

Please. The only time I felt free and liberated was on my bike. "I feel blocked," I said.

"Imagine your spirit soaring," Lupe counseled.

Sure. But what did my spirit look like?

"Now, what insights have you all gained?" Lupe asked.

Again with the psychobabble.

"I'm repressed," Tyler said.

Maybe he longed to be a Barbie-shaped woman?

"I don't let people in," Skyler said. In where—her McMansion?

When my turn came, I gazed upon my tableau. It depicted what looked like a green water bottle melting onto a tabletop, à la Salvador Dalí. "I'm hot and thirsty," I said. None of that Freudian mumbo-jumbo for me.

Shortly afterward, Lupe wrapped things up, and the group shuffled out, proudly carrying their creations. Once they were discharged from The Oasis, they'd no doubt have their works placed under preservation glass, triple-matted, and encased in gilded wood frames.

After everyone left, I lingered to talk to Lupe. I hadn't seen her since shortly after my admission, and I knew she'd be concerned about my welfare. Plus, I hoped she could provide some insights into the bizarre things I'd uncovered.

To my disappointment, she was unable to provide any helpful information. She had not been aware that the victims had all attended the same school. Nor did she have a clue as to why someone might have stashed printed materials in the restroom ceiling. And she didn't know the identity of the mysterious "acquanaturale," who had sent the celeb pics to the *Inquisitor.*

"I feel like this afternoon has been a waste," I said.

"Don't be so sure," Lupe said, laying a hand on my shoulder. "Perhaps this afternoon's activity will yield some answers for you. Your subconscious holds some keys already, but that knowledge needs to bubble up into your awareness."

"Oh . . . kay," I said. I didn't dispute the theory, just the method.

"Stay safe, *chica*," Lupe said.

"Count on it."

I RETURNED TO my room. Still no message from Enrique. The toilet cam seemed like another waste. I collapsed onto the bed, exhausted. I'd barely slept in two nights. I'd just take a short power nap, then get back on the case.

ROME. AGAIN. THE Piazza Navona. Sitting al fresco at a trattoria. Families taking their evening passagiata, flaunting their fashions and footwear. Pigeons fluttering. The scent of fresh-baked pizza. Bruce beside me, holding my hand.

A waiter appears.

"Buona sera, signori. Can I get you some bottled water? Acqua frizzante *or* acqua naturale?" *He looks at me expectantly.*

I look to Bruce. "I'm sorry, I don't understand what he means."

Bruce withdraws his hand. The candlelight from the table bounces off his black pupils.

"What did I pay that Italian tutor for all summer? Were you studying—or screwing him?"

He turns to the waiter. "Tutti e due, per favore. *Both, please.*"

"Sì, signore."

Bruce glares at me until the waiter returns with two green glass water bottles. The waiter opens them, pours a glass from each bottle, then leaves again. Bruce grabs one of the glasses and holds it up. Bubbles rise to the surface. "Acqua frizzante. *Sparkling water.*"

He lifts up the glass, turns it, and pours the water over my head.

He grabs the other glass and pours that one on me.

"Acqua naturale. *Still water.*"

I awoke, drenched.

Still water. I remembered Dr. Stillwater complaining about missing her annual vacation to Italy because of the deaths at The Oasis. She was an Italiophile. She was "acquanaturale."

Chapter 17

THE PHOTOS OF Cody Keys and Jordan Mitchell had been e-mailed to the *Inquisitor* from Dr. Stillwater's account. Had she sent them herself, betraying her own patients' confidentiality? If so, why?

Most likely, to get publicity for The Oasis. Everyone would want to go where the stars went for treatment. Stillwater must have figured that the potential gains from the media attention outweighed the loss of The Oasis's reputation for discretion. And she was probably right. Celebrity discretion meant dick these days. Disease and dysfunction were often assets rather than liabilities.

But there went my idea that it was the teen victims who'd leaked the photos and that someone had killed them to shut them down. It was yet another dead end in this investigation, added to the toilet cam that hadn't revealed anyone accessing the hidden reading stash. On top of that, my theory that the victims had double-crossed Shrimp Pimp had gone down the drain, too—at least if Shrimp Pimp was to be believed that the teens had expressed complete disinterest in drugs or sex.

I was getting nowhere at The Oasis. My only remaining hope was at the school, with Lars.

I rose unsteadily from the bed. The nightmare had shaken me. I headed for the restroom to take a shower to clear my body and mind. Before I could reach it, though, there was a frantic pounding on the door.

"Harriet! Harriet!" Gitta's panicked voice came from the other side.

I opened the door. Gitta stood there, eyes wide, blonde hair askew. Daniel stood behind her, his hands on her shoulders.

"Mrs. Castellano, calm down. There's no Harriet here. This is Hailey."

"Let go of me!" Gitta snarled, slapping at Daniel.

She grabbed my arm. "It's Lars. He just called me in my room. He said he was in the school kitchen, and he thought someone was following him. Then the call was dropped. I kept calling back, but his phone just kept ringing and then going to voice mail. Something terrible has happened to my baby!"

I felt my own panic rising. Maybe there was nothing to be alarmed about. But I couldn't take that chance. Dammit, dammit, dammit. I should never have let the kid go into that school. What the hell had I been thinking?

"Call Detective Reilly of the Boca Police," I snapped at Daniel. I no longer cared about blowing my cover with Reilly. All I cared about was Lars. And Gitta needed Reilly by her side.

"Tell Reilly what she just said," I told Daniel. "Have him meet us at the school. Sterling Heights Academy."

"But . . . but . . ." Daniel sputtered.

"Do it!" I grabbed Gitta by the elbow. "We're outta here."

I grabbed my Harley key from my nightstand and ran through the halls of The Oasis, dragging Gitta behind me on her high heels. Ignoring all the staff who tried to stop us, we rushed to the front entrance, burst out, and ran across the lawn to the parking lot.

My Hog sat where I'd parked it—had it been just two days before?

I took my helmet off the backrest, dug my leather jacket out of the saddlebag, and handed the gear to Gitta. I hated to ride without protection, but I had no choice. We had to get to Lars.

We straddled the bike, Gitta perching precariously behind me, grasping her arms around my waist so tight I could barely breathe. I stuck the key in the ignition and pushed the starter button. The bike roared like a lion awakened from slumber. Shifting into first, I opened up the throttle and let out the clutch. We thundered past the guard gate and onto the street. The wind rushed past my body as the engine rumbled, the frame vibrated, and the road spread before me. God, it felt good to be in charge again, unconstrained by institutional structures.

I remembered the school's address from the computer records I'd hacked. It was a couple miles away in an old section of town. I headed in that direction, Gitta screaming "Hurry!" in my ear. Like I didn't get that.

Twilight had descended, and with it, the day's heat and humidity had waned. Car headlights and taillights twinkled across the roads. The lights in Boca's sleek glass office buildings were turning off, while those in the Spanish-tile-roofed houses and balconied condos were coming on.

We tore through town, weaving through rush-hour traffic, veering onto sidewalks, and running red lights. In ten minutes we pulled up to Sterling Heights Academy.

Its appearance did not live up to its noble name. The building was a three-story elongated structure, its red bricks blackened with grime. Weak lighting illuminated the windows from within. Surveillance cameras were mounted on each corner of the rooftop and above the entrance. A metal fence with barbed wire across the top surrounded the building. On the scraggly front lawn, a plastic sign with missing letters spelled out "St_r_ing Hei_ht_ Ac_d_my." The place looked more like a prison than a school.

The building and grounds appeared deserted. The cops were nowhere in sight. In that bumper-to-bumper traffic, even a patrol car with lights flashing and sirens blaring wouldn't have made it as fast as we had on the Hog.

We rolled up to the front entrance. Gitta pried her fingers from my abs, where I figured her nails had left permanent indentations. We dismounted, and Gitta pulled off her helmet. Her hair lay plastered to her head. We sprinted to the door, Gitta darting as gracefully as a gazelle in her high heels. I pulled the door handle. Locked.

"Omigod," Gitta wailed. "What are we going to do?"

I looked through the thick, wire-reinforced glass insert in the top half of the door. A long hallway lined with lockers stretched ahead, empty. I reached into my boot and pulled out my snub-nose .44 Magnum. "Step back," I ordered Gitta.

I grabbed the gun in both hands like a baseball bat and swung the butt into the glass. My shoulder cracked, while the glass barely did. There had to be a better way.

I looked again into the door's window, and seeing no one in the hallway, I fired into the glass. It shattered inward. Alarm bells shrieked.

I shoved the gun back into my boot. "Let me have my jacket back," I said to Gitta.

She handed me the jacket. I shrugged into it, then stuck my arm between the edges of the jagged glass, reached down, and unlocked the deadbolt. I retracted my arm, pulled open the door, and we entered into a high-ceilinged lobby.

A wooden doorway marked "Office" was on our left. A dimly lit main corridor spread before us, and another lay to the right. Where the hell would the kitchen be? Probably somewhere around the perimeter of the building.

"Come on," I said, and we rushed down the main corridor, my boots clomping on the cement floor, Gitta's stiletto sandals clattering, and the alarms clanging. The hallway reeked of stale sneakers and cheap floor polish. That and the sight of rows of grey metal lockers lining the sickly-green walls gave me the creeps. I hadn't set foot in a high school since my own early escape at seventeen, and my memories of my alma mater, with its Boca Babes-in-training, were not particularly fond ones.

At the end of the hallway, a posted sign read "Cafeteria" with an arrow pointing to the right. We ran that way and burst through a set of swinging doors into the lunchroom. Another set of double doors was at the far end, next to a conveyor belt for trays. Dodging around tables, we rushed to that entrance. Just as I reached the doors, my foot slipped on something and flew out from under me. I fell on my ass.

What the hell? I looked around on the floor—there was no water or anything else slippery. I sat up and examined the sole of my boot. A small torn piece of cardstock paper was stuck to it. Black lettering on it spelled out "bo Bra."

Shit. I peeled off the paper, tossed it aside, scrambled to my feet, and rushed through the double doors, Gitta on my heels.

The kitchen smelled of old grease and Pine Sol. An industrial stove, grill, and stainless steel counters and sinks spread before us.

I surveyed the room. A tall metal storage rack stood against one wall, stocked with twelve-ounce plastic Coca-Cola bottles. Next to it, I saw a pair of large metal doors with an embossed name reading "Arctic Freeze." The wooden shaft of a rag mop was shoved through the handles of the doors. And a shattered cell phone lay at the doors' base.

Oh my God—someone had tried to kill Lars by trapping him in the walk-in freezer. Jesus, what if we were too late to save him?

"Over there!" I yelled, pointing at the freezer.

We clambered across the tile floor. My hip hit one of the sinks. I went down, tripping Gitta. She tumbled on top of me, and a dish rack came down on both of us. Gitta screamed.

"Shit!" I said. I shoved aside the dish rack, sending it clattering across the floor. Gitta's elbow punched my stomach as she tried to rise. I gasped for breath, then grabbed her shoulders and rolled both of us onto our sides. I got onto all fours, then stood and pulled Gitta up by the hand.

We rushed to the freezer. I pulled out the mop and swung the heavy door open. A blast of cold air hit us.

Lars was slumped along the far wall in a fetal position. The hood of his sweatshirt enveloped his head. His left hand was tucked inside his opposite armpit, and his right hand clutched an unopened plastic Coke bottle.

"Baby!" Gitta screamed.

I dove to him. His lips were blue, his skin translucent, and his teeth chattered. I grabbed his feet and dragged him toward the entrance. He remained curled. Gitta maneuvered behind him and pushed as I pulled. We got him out of the freezer just as I heard sirens in the distance.

"Mom," Lars mumbled.

"It's okay, baby," Gitta said, stroking his forehead. "I'm here now. You're going to be okay."

"We need to huddle around him," I said. "Transfer our body heat."

Gitta wrapped her arms and legs around him on one side, and I did the same on the other, sandwiching him between us.

The sirens outside got louder, then abruptly stopped.

"C . . . c . . . coke," Lars mumbled.

Gitta and I looked at each other.

"C-coke," he repeated. His hand still clutched the Coke bottle.

"You want a drink of your Coke?" I asked.

He shook his head violently. "Mi . . . Miss . . . La . . . Fleur," he stammered. "Prin . . . principal. Ser . . . served C-coke."

"Shh, Lars," Gitta said. "You don't need to talk now."

But he continued. "W . . . went to . . . get . . . Coke . . . in . . . kitchen. G-got . . . sh-shoved . . . in."

I heard a stampede of footsteps.

I slipped the Coke bottle out of Lars's fingers and into my jacket pocket just as Detective Reilly, accompanied by Officers Hernandez and Fernandez and two paramedics, burst through the kitchen's swinging doors.

"Kevin!" Gitta screamed.

Reilly reached us in two strides. He crouched and gently pried Gitta's fingers off Lars. "It's okay, sweetheart," he said. "Let the medics handle it now."

"What happened?" one of the paramedics asked.

"We found him in the walk-in freezer," I said. "He said he was pushed in."

Lars shivered as I kept myself pressed against him.

"How long was he in there?" the paramedic asked.

"About half an hour," I said. It had been that long since Gitta had received the call from Lars saying someone was following him in the kitchen.

"Okay, please step back and let us work," the other paramedic said.

Reluctantly, I unwrapped myself from around Lars. I felt like I was failing to protect him. Hell, I *had* failed.

Gitta, Reilly, and I rose. The paramedics lifted Lars onto a gurney, bundled him in heating packs and blankets, started an IV and oxygen flow, strapped him down, then rolled him out to a waiting ambulance to take him to East Boca Hospital.

Reilly turned to me. "I'm going to escort Gitta outside to ride in the ambulance with Lars. But I want to talk to you. Don't move. I'll be right back."

Like I could move with Hernandez and Fernandez there.

When Reilly returned, his face was as red as his hair. "So you're at it again, Horowitz," he said. "Messing in police business. Gitta just now told me all about your little undercover operation at The Oasis and how Lars ended up in here." His voice rose. "I could have you arrested for interfering with a police investigation. And endangering the welfare of a minor." He leaned in closer to me. "And this is personal. I'm going to marry that woman, although she doesn't know that yet. That's my future stepson we're talking about."

"Reilly," I sighed, "there's nothing you can say that will make me feel worse than I already do. Let's set aside our bickering. We've got bigger things to focus on."

"Agreed." He turned to the uniforms. "Fernandez, secure the scene. Hernandez, call the crime scene techs. I'm going to the hospital to get the boy's statement."

"I'll meet you there," I said. I had two reasons to be at the hospital: Lars. And Lior.

Outside, I straddled my bike and took off, still recriminating myself about Lars. And about Gardenia LaFleur. All this time I'd thought she was the kids' foster mother, because she had called them her "children." But according to Lars, she was the principal of Sterling Heights.

I remembered the news report I'd seen on TV about the principals' convention at the Boca Beach Hilton. One of the principals who was interviewed had spoken of her "kids." The word wasn't literal—it was commonly used by teachers and principals as an expression of their feelings for their students. I'd been an idiot to make an unfounded assumption.

Who knew what I could have accomplished by now on this case— not to mention sparing Lior and Lars—if not for that stupid mistake. I could have been checking out the school from the start, instead of going on wild goose chases after Social Climber, Stillwater, and Shrimp Pimp at The Oasis. In anger, I flicked my right wrist to speed up the bike, changed lanes, and roared down the road.

Rush hour had come and gone while we'd dealt with life and death, and traffic on the Boca streets now flowed at a steady pace. My Hog pulsated its rhythmic vibe as the pavement rolled underneath my feet. Soon, my heart began to beat in sync with the pistons. As it often did, the bike transported not only my body, but my mind into a different dimension.

And that's when everything fell into place, and I realized what had really happened to the kids at The Oasis.

Chapter 18

I ARRIVED AT THE hospital facing an agonizing decision—should I see Lior or Lars first? Both had been victimized because of me. But now I also knew who had tried to kill them. And why. So the person I really needed to see was Reilly.

I pulled up to the ER entrance, parked the Hog, and rushed inside the sliding glass doors. The waiting room was nearly filled with people in various degrees of distress, from dozing to dazed. I ran to the front desk, which was manned by . . . well, a man. It's not like I was in a state of mind to take note of his features and fashion. He was a faceless bureaucrat. But when it came to dealing with bureaucrats, I knew from past experience that my habitual Dirty Harry demeanor would likely be perceived as belligerent, so I did my best to tamp down my agitation.

"Hi," I said. "A young man was just brought in—Lars O'Malley. A police detective is probably with him. I'd like to go speak to the detective, please."

"And you would be . . ."

"Harriet Horowitz, a friend of the family."

"I'm sorry, but only family members are allowed back in the treatment bays."

I took a deep breath to keep from blowing my stack. "Perhaps you could ask Detective Reilly if he could come out here to speak with me for a moment? It's urgent police business."

"Certainly I can ask." He picked up a phone on the desk and relayed the message. "The detective will be right out."

Gee, maybe I really needed to use the diplomatic approach more often.

Reilly strode out of the treatment area into the waiting room, a scowl on his face. "What is it, Horowitz? I'm a little busy here."

I ignored the sarcasm in his tone. "How's Lars?"

"Lying under a pile of electric blankets and warming lamps. He'll recover, but he's in no shape to talk now."

I let out a sigh of relief. "I have some information for you. Can we go over to the corner where it's more private?"

Reilly rolled his eyes but followed me to an alcove in the far corner of the room. We stood facing each other.

"I know who trapped Lars in that freezer," I said.

Reilly raised his eyebrows.

"Gardenia LaFleur, the school principal."

"And what makes you say that?"

"Because Lars figured out that Gardenia had spiked the kids' Coke. So she had to kill him."

"She spiked their Coke—with what, alcohol?"

"No, a stimulant—Turbo Brain. It's a liquid supplement that improves focus and concentration. I saw an ad for it on TV."

"Why would Gardenia do that?"

"To improve their reading scores. According to the Contessa, reading scores on standardized tests at Sterling Heights Academy have shot up miraculously since Gardenia LaFleur took over as principal. Here's how I think she did that. During reading classes, she served Coke—laced with Turbo Brain. I think she was giving them high doses—much more than the couple drops that are recommended. So the kids got addicted to the drug—and it's almost like they got addicted to Coke and reading, too. It's the whole conditioned and unconditioned stimulus-response thing."

Reilly looked at me like I had antennae springing from my head.

"Bear with me, Reilly. Here are some facts. One"—I raised my index finger—"Demarcus, the murder victim, was found clutching a torn half of a phone book and an empty Coke bottle. Two"—middle finger—"Jessica and Amber, the girls who fought in the dining room, were arguing over a Coke bottle. Three"—ring finger—"reading materials have been disappearing from The Oasis—menus, brochures, everything. Four"—pinky—"I found a stash of printed materials hidden in the air-conditioning vent of a restroom at The Oasis. And five"—thumb—"just now in the school cafeteria I slipped on a piece of card stock that said 'bo Bra.' That wasn't from a bra—it was torn from a package of Turbo Brain. Gardenia must have dropped it in her rush to get out of the kitchen after she shoved Lars in the freezer."

Reilly stared at me, looking incredulous.

"Don't you see?" I grabbed his forearm. "The kids were in withdrawal. They were craving Turbo Brain—except they didn't know that. From their perspective, what they were craving was Coke and reading, since that's what they associated with feeling ultra-focused, ultra-energetic, ultra-alert. So they fought—and killed—over access to Coke and reading material."

Reilly shook his head. "Speculation, Horowitz. Pure, wild, speculation."

I dug my fingers further into his forearm. "Those kids had no trace of drugs in their systems. Why? Because normal drug screening doesn't test for Turbo Brain. No one realized what the kids were actually addicted to."

"Horowitz, you have a fevered imagination. I, on the other hand, have a real investigation to conduct." He pulled his arm away and turned to go.

"Wait. Just wait. Let me explain."

"You have been explaining, if that's what you call it."

"Just give me one more minute. One minute—that's all."

He sighed dramatically. "Fine. One minute. That's it."

"Okay, look. Lior was attacked last night at The Oasis. He was injected with some kind of stimulant. But the doctors didn't know what—again, because Turbo Brain wouldn't show up on normal blood and urine screens."

"Yeah, I heard about Lior's attack at this morning's police briefing. Actually I wondered what your man was doing there with some woman named Hailey. Now I know."

I ignored that. "I think Gardenia is the one who attacked Lior. I saw her twice at The Oasis. She was acting grief-stricken, but that was probably a cover for her to snoop around to see if anyone was onto her. Last night, Lior and I were in the Meditation Maze. I'd stake my life that Gardenia was there, too."

"And why do you say that?"

"Because earlier that day, I heard Dr. Stillwater encourage Gardenia to go for a walk on the grounds. So I bet that in the maze, Gardenia overheard me tell Lior what was going on at The Oasis. She saw that I posed a threat. She tried to kill me but missed and got Lior instead."

"So she just happened to have a hypodermic needle with this Turbo Brain on her?"

"I heard Gardenia tell Stillwater that she used insulin shots—so she must have a supply of needles and syringes. That's how she injected Lior, and I bet that's how she got the Turbo Brain into the Coke bottles. By injecting it—probably through the plastic bottle caps."

"And how do you figure Lars found this out?"

"He's a health nut, right? He wouldn't go near a Coke bottle with a ten-foot pole. But he must have been in a class where he saw Gardenia serve Coke to the other kids. Then he would have seen its effects on them. Alertness, eagerness, excitement . . . who acts like that in a class-room normally?"

Reilly grunted.

"Lars has lived with a cocaine-addicted mother all his life," I said. "Cocaine is a stimulant. So he'd know the signs when he saw them. Just now at the school, he told me he'd gone to the kitchen to get a Coke bottle. Why would he do that since he doesn't drink the stuff? It had to be because he wanted to have it analyzed to prove his suspicion. Gardenia followed him and shoved him into the freezer."

"Okay, Horowitz. Your one minute is up." Reilly turned to leave.

"Here!" I pulled the Coke bottle out of my leather jacket pocket. "This is the evidence." I shoved it up to his face. "Lars was holding this when we found him. Have it tested. I'm telling you, you'll find Turbo Brain."

"Horowitz, even if I had the slightest belief in this cockamamie story you've cooked up, your so-called evidence wouldn't mean a thing. Even if it's true that Lars was holding it, as you say, you, Miss Private Detective, have bypassed any evidential chain of custody by taking it from him. *If* it were to contain this Turbo Brain, there's no way to prove you didn't put it in there yourself."

Shit. He was right.

"Besides," Reilly went on, "as you said, this stuff isn't picked up by normal tests. We'd have to send it to the state lab—and in case you haven't heard while living in your fantasy world, they have a backlog of weeks. Now, I've heard enough from your crazed imagination. I'm going back to see if the actual victim can give me any information now."

I watched him walk away, mentally kicking myself in the ass. God-dammit. I collapsed onto a leather chair and buried my head in my hands.

Now what? Once Lars told Reilly what he'd mumbled to me about Gardenia and the Coke bottle, Reilly would probably go to question Gardenia. But she'd just lie and slip through his fingers. I couldn't let that happen. Okay . . . if I couldn't prove my theory to Reilly, at least I could prove it to myself. And I knew who just might be able to help me get that proof. Leonard, Mom's paramour and ex-CIA agent. Poisoning was a threat that spies faced all the time—so the agency could well have a secret field test kit that would detect any substance known to man.

I felt my back pocket for my cell phone. It wasn't there. Oh yeah, it was still at The Oasis. I walked up to the receptionist at the front desk. "Could I please make a phone call?"

"There's a courtesy phone over there." He pointed to a side table along a wall.

I reached it in a couple strides and picked up the receiver.

Of course, I didn't have Leonard's number in my mental memory. But I did have Mom's home number, since that hadn't changed since I'd lived there as a kid. I called the house, hoping Leonard would be there. I didn't want to deal with Mom and all her inevitable questions. Thankfully, Leonard himself answered after a couple rings. Good—now dealing with Mom would be his problem.

"Leonard, it's me, Harriet. I'm at East Boca Medical Center."

"Are you all right?"

"Yes, I'm fine. But I need your help."

"At your service. What can I do?"

"I need to have the contents of a Coke bottle analyzed for an unusual stimulant—not the typical stuff that a normal drug test would detect."

"No problem."

We arranged to meet in the hospital's parking lot in fifteen minutes. Awesome. Mom had hooked a good one this time. And this gave me time to go see Lior.

I returned to the front desk.

"I'd like to visit a patient," I told the guy there. "The Contessa von Phul has arranged for him to stay in the Presidential Suite." It never hurt to drop the Contessa's name. "Can you tell me which way it is?"

"I'm sorry, what was your name again?"

"Harriet Horowitz."

He tapped his keyboard and stared at his screen. "I see that the Contessa has put you on the patient's visitors list. But the patient is no longer here."

"What?"

"He's been discharged."

And he hadn't called me? Oh yeah, I didn't have my phone, so maybe he had. And dammit, his number was stored in there—not in my brain. So I couldn't call him. Well, the good news was that he must be recovered, since he'd been discharged. I'd see him just as soon as I saw this case through to its bitter end.

I walked outside to wait for Leonard. Taking a seat on a bench underneath the lighted portico, I pulled the Coke bottle from my jacket to examine the cap for a needle puncture. I couldn't see one. In fact, I couldn't see the cap clearly at all. The white writing on the red background was tiny. I moved to try to find better lighting. That didn't help. I moved the bottle closer, then further, from my eyes, but that didn't bring it into focus either. I gave up.

I wondered why Gardenia hadn't taken the bottle from Lars. Probably in the heat of the moment, all she wanted was to deep-freeze him. Plus, she couldn't afford a struggle—the odds were against her. Lars was a fit kid, while Gardenia was an overweight, diabetic, older woman.

I watched the headlights of cars entering the parking lot. At last, I saw Leonard's classic red '63 Corvette Stingray pull in. He drove up to where I sat and leaned over to push the passenger door open for me. I climbed in.

Leonard's gray eyes, which matched his silver brush-cut hair, gleamed. Clearly, the man was thrilled to be on the case.

He pulled into a parking spot away from the building and snapped on the overhead light. "Let's get to work," he said.

No whys or whats. That was Leonard—straight to the point, no questions asked.

I handed him the Coke bottle. "First of all, can you see any pinprick in that cap?"

"Not without my reading glasses." He pulled a silver-rimmed pair out of the breast pocket of his shirt, perched it on his nose, then took a look. "Sure enough," he said. "You can't see it?"

"No, I guess it's too small."

He peered at me over the top of his glasses. "Here, try these." He took off the glasses and handed them to me.

Say what?

I grabbed them, shoved them on, and looked. The bottle cap was now crystal clear. In its center was a tiny round hole. Oh my god . . . Dirty Harriet needed reading glasses. What an indignity on the eve of my fortieth birthday. "Let's get this stuff tested," I snapped, returning the glasses.

Leonard reached behind his seat to the little storage area that was there in place of a back seat and pulled out a hard-sided briefcase. He set the briefcase on his lap, flipped it open, and removed a small laptop. "Here, you hold onto this," he said, handing it to me.

"Now this here"—he patted a weird-looking metal box which was connected by a plastic tube to a glass jar, all within the briefcase—"is a portable, high-performance, liquid chromatography system. It analyzes . . ."

Please. Spare me the chemistry lesson.

"Great!" I cut him off. "So . . ."

"So you turn that computer on."

That much I could do. I pressed the power button.

Leonard hooked a USB cable from the laptop to the metal box. "All right, give me the solvent," he said.

"Solvent?"

"The Coke bottle."

"Oh." I handed it to him.

He poured the contents into the glass jar, then flipped some switches on the box. It hummed. Reaching across me, he tapped some keys on the laptop.

"This software contains a database of just about every pharmacological and toxic agent on the planet," Leonard said. "So the molecular compounds of your liquid will be compared to the database for a match."

The metal box stopped humming, and the laptop beeped.

"There you go," Leonard said.

A line graph consisting of a series of red, orange, and yellow spikes appeared on the screen. What the hell did that mean?

Then a smaller window popped up labeled "Chemical Composition." The first item listed was "Coca-Cola: 50%." This was followed by a long list of scientific mumbo jumbo. Great, that wasn't much help.

Okay, wait. I just had to compare this list with the ingredients of Turbo Brain.

"Leonard, can I borrow your phone?" I asked.

"Sure," he said, handing it over.

I Googled Turbo Brain. "Our product is a proprietary blend that includes . . ." All the items on that list also appeared on the laptop. Of course, the Turbo Brain site did not include the proportions of each ingredient, nor all the components, since that was a trade secret. But what was there matched.

I knew it! Gardenia must have used her syringe to withdraw half the Coke from the bottle and replace it with Turbo Brain. That was a hell of a bigger dose than two drops. "Thanks, Leonard." I gave him a kiss on the cheek. "You're the best."

"Anytime, Harriet. By the way, you know you must never mention this equipment to anyone."

"Yes, of course. I'll handle the rest from here," I said. Or rather, my Inner Vigilante would. That goddamn Gardenia was pure evil. And I was going to bring her down. I bet I knew where to find her, too.

I got out of the car and tramped back into the hospital lobby to the courtesy phone. A woman was just hanging up. Good for her, because my Inner Vigilante did not possess patience as character trait.

I needed Enrique's number . . . and it sprang to my mind immediately. When my Inner Vigilante was loose, my mental acuity was laser-sharp. I might need reading glasses, but I still had my edge when it mattered. I punched in the numbers, and Enrique picked up.

"That school principals' convention," I said. "Is it still going on at your hotel?"

"Well, hello to you, too," he said.

"Just answer, please."

"What's the matter with you?"

"Nothing's the matter with me. Convention—happening?"

"Yes. They're having a closing banquet in the ballroom right now."

"Is there a Gardenia LaFleur registered?"

I heard keys tapping. "Uh-huh."

I hung up and strode outside to my Hog. I was ready to kill that bitch.

Chapter 19

I RUMBLED ALONG the mean streets of Boca. The engine's revolutions throbbed in my ears, and I felt every pebble in the road. The sky was now pitch-black. The lights of oncoming cars radiated bursts of incandescence. I zigzagged through traffic with a flick of my wrist and a shift of my body weight. Up ahead loomed the tall tower of the Boca Beach Hilton, the lights in its windows shimmering like constellations in the night.

I pulled right onto the walkway by the front entrance, shut down the bike, took off my helmet, and marched in, ignoring the squawks of the valet behind me.

I'd been in the place before, so I knew where the ballroom was. I headed straight for it, passing guests and staff in the hallway. I heard the laughter and the clinking of glasses and silverware before I burst through the carved double door.

Round tables occupied by diners filled the space, draped with white tablecloths and stacked with half-eaten meals. Smells of baked chicken and fish turned my stomach. I hadn't set foot in a ballroom since I'd shot Bruce in front of five hundred witnesses at a wedding reception. Fear of reliving that trauma had kept me away. Now, I didn't care.

The guests chattered like chipmunks, taking no notice of me. I scanned the tables, row by row. There she was, holding court at a table right in the middle of the room. The miracle worker who had elevated at-risk kids into the academic stratosphere. She wore a royal purple suit, with a matching purse hanging from the back of her chair. Her face was animated as all eyes at the table were on her. She looked nothing like the grief-stricken mother figure I'd seen at The Oasis.

Rage rose from my gut to my chest to my head and propelled me to her. This woman had caused the deaths of innocent children. All for power and glory. And hell, for all I knew, money—maybe she was skimming from the grants her school received as reward for its stellar performance.

By the time I reached her, I had reined in my rage just enough to say, "Ms. LaFleur, may I have a word?"

"What is this in reference to?" she asked, looking around at her tablemates.

"You might prefer to discuss it in private," I said. I had no desire to cause another scene in a ballroom.

"Who are you?" Gardenia said.

Okay, I guess she wasn't budging from her throne. We'd have to have it out right there before an audience. "Well, Gardenia," I said, "I'm the one you tried to kill in the Meditation Maze. But you missed."

There was a collective gasp around the table.

"And I know all about the Turbo Brain in the Coke," I said. "What you did to those poor kids."

"What are you talking about?" Gardenia said.

"You know damn well what I'm talking about. You tried to hook your 'children' on reading by pairing it with huge doses of Turbo Brain. Unbeknowst to them. And hey, it worked great in the short term. The students read voraciously, and their reading scores skyrocketed."

The tablemates started whispering.

"But guess what?" I snarled. "Substance use has a way of getting nasty in the long term. Dependence reared its ugly head. Your 'kids' lost interest in anything but getting their next fix. They got no pleasure from food, for one thing. That's why one of them died of anorexia while at The Oasis."

Gardenia glared at me.

"They didn't care about sports or sex, either," I said. "You know, normal adolescent interests. That's why your lacrosse team sucked. And why none of them could be bothered with sex while at The Oasis."

"Young lady, you are making no sense," Gardenia said, her voice rising.

The whole room went silent.

I barreled right on. "Oh, and then there's the little withdrawal problem. Another of your 'kids' died from seizures."

The chatter started up again.

But I wasn't done. "Then there was the final straw—violence. Once the kids were in The Oasis, they were no longer getting Turbo Brain. Which meant they weren't getting their expected stimulation from Coke and reading. They thought they needed more and more of those things to get their "high." So they fought over possession of those items and hoarded them. And ultimately one of the kids—I don't who yet—killed Demarcus over a Coke bottle and a phone book."

Gardenia looked around at her table companions, who were staring at her. As was everyone else in the room. "This woman is a patient from The Oasis," she said. "She's obviously mentally disturbed."

"Like hell," I said. "It's over, Gardenia. The boy you shoved in the freezer today? Guess what? He's not dead. He's told the police he saw you serving Coke in the classroom, and how the kids reacted. And the cops have seized all the adulterated Coke bottles from the school."

Okay, so that was a lie. But it fooled Gardenia. Her body folded in on itself, and her face went slack and ashen. Suddenly, she looked once again like the bereaved caretaker.

"I never meant to hurt my kids," she sobbed. "I did it for them. They came to love reading. What principal—or parent—wouldn't want that for their children?"

"Bullshit," I said. "You did it for yourself. To get the glory of being a star principal. To reap the rewards of fame and fortune. You didn't care what it did to the kids."

"No, that's not true," she cried. "I didn't know they would develop all those awful reactions. Once I saw the terrible effects, I made sure that our school counselor got them into treatment. And I visited them there every day to see how they were doing."

"Oh, you're a saint," I said. "You had them sent to treatment. You just didn't bother to inform anyone what they were addicted to."

Gardenia reached into her purse and started to rise from her chair. "Liar!" she yelled. When she stood and withdrew her hand, her fingers gripped a needle and syringe. She lunged at me, needle aloft.

The guests screamed.

Suddenly, I was in another ballroom.

The wedding reception. Five hundred guests. Chandeliers gleaming, silverware tinkling. Then Bruce lunges at me with his fist. The guests scream. I grab the Magnum and aim it at him . . .

I reached into my boot, pulled out my Magnum, and aimed it at Gardenia.

More screams erupted throughout the room. The seated guests reeled back from the table, sending their chairs toppling.

Then a voice shouted, "Drop your weapons!"

Chapter 20

QUICKLY SWEEPING my eyes around, I took in Enrique, Reilly, and the two uniforms, Hernandez and Fernandez, surrounding us. All three cops had their weapons drawn.

I dropped my gun to the floor and raised my hands.

Gardenia stumbled backward into her chair. Her fingers loosened, and the needle and syringe fell from her grasp.

"Cuff her, Hernandez," Reilly said.

Hernandez took a step toward me.

"No, not her," Reilly said. "Her!" He pointed at Gardenia. "Gardenia LaFleur, you are under arrest for multiple counts of child abuse, the attempted murder of Harriet Horowitz, the attempted murder of Lars O'Malley, and the aggravated assault of Lior ben Yehuda."

He recited her Miranda rights as Hernandez cuffed her hands behind her back. Fernandez donned a pair of gloves, picked up the needle and syringe, and placed them in an evidence bag. Then Hernandez hauled Gardenia off as she sobbed, "My children! My children!"

"Those of you at this table, stay here," Reilly said. "Officer Fernandez will take your statements." He walked to the front of the ballroom, ascended a podium that was there, and grabbed a microphone from atop it. A whining squeal boomed from the speakers. Guests cringed and covered their ears. After the noise subsided, Reilly announced, "Folks, the party's over. Please leave the room in an orderly manner."

A hubbub ensued as the crowd did as instructed.

I sank heavily into Gardenia's vacated chair. Enrique pushed a glass of water toward me, and I gulped down the liquid.

"How did you . . . ," I asked Enrique after I'd swallowed the glassful.

"You didn't sound like yourself when you called me," he said. "I mean, you're normally bitchy, but this time there was an extra edge in your voice."

Other women might have taken offense at that, but I knew I was a bitch on wheels . . . and proud of it.

"I knew something big had to be going down," Enrique said. "And when I saw you enter the hotel on my security cam, I figured you were after Gardenia, since you'd asked about her. So I came after you. I got here just as the cops arrived. Are you okay?"

I nodded. "Thanks, pal."

Reilly returned to the table. "Horowitz, you're coming to the police station with me. I need a full statement from you."

"Why did you come here?" I asked him.

"Lars recovered sufficiently to tell me what happened at the school. His account corroborated what you told me. I made some quick inquiries to establish Ms. LaFleur's whereabouts and found out she was here. So I came to arrest her. Which would have gone off just fine without your theatrics. Now let's go."

"Lior," I said. "I need to see Lior."

"Later," Reilly said. "You're coming with me now."

I SPENT THE NEXT I-don't-know-how-many hours in a windowless room at police headquarters, detailing for the record what I'd hastily told Reilly at the hospital. At least he had the heart to provide coffee and Tylenol. They went down bitter.

Reilly looked like he wasn't faring much better. His copper hair stuck out in spikes, and his eyes were bloodshot.

As we were finally wrapping up, a knock came at the door.

"Yeah," Reilly called.

Fernandez stuck his head in the doorway. "May I have a word with you, Detective?"

"Excuse me a moment, Horowitz," Reilly said.

As if I had a choice.

The fluorescent light overhead flickered, making my eyeballs hurt. I felt so alone. No Lior. No Enrique. No Contessa or Lupe. Not even Gitta or Slick or Lana. I laid my head down on my arms atop the ornate carved oak table. Yeah, an oak table in a police interview room. This was Boca.

I heard the door open and looked up to see Reilly re-enter.

"Okay, Harriet," he said with a sigh. Harriet? He always called me Horowitz.

"Based on your statement, we corroborated that there were only two other kids from Sterling Heights Academy at The Oasis at the time of Demarcus's murder."

"Jessica Jarrett and the girl who stabbed her with a fork, Amber Moss."

"Right. Amber is in custody, so we had her fingerprints. I was able to get a warrant for Jessica's prints, which Fernandez then got from her at the hospital."

"And?"

"Jessica's prints matched a set of previously unidentified prints found on the hedge clippers that Demarcus was stabbed with. The same prints were also found on the phone book and the stash of printed material in the restroom."

Oh my god. No wonder the person who'd stashed the materials in the restroom had never shown up on Enrique's toilet cam—she'd been in the hospital the whole time, being treated for her stab wound.

"I've sent Hernandez to guard Jessica's room so she doesn't escape," Reilly said. "I'm going to the hospital now to talk with her. You're free to go, Harriet."

"Yeah," I said, rising from my seat. "Free to go with you to see this girl."

Reilly sighed. "All right. Come on. You did help crack the case."

Help? I *did* crack the case. But I decided to keep my mouth shut while I was ahead.

JESSICA JARRETT looked tiny in her hospital bed, swaddled in linens like a baby, bandages taped around her throat, a plastic IV tube slithering out of a tattooed arm, her dyed-red dreadlocks drooping around her pale, freckled face.

The clock on the wall opposite her head read two a.m. The girl should have been asleep. Instead, she had a magazine propped in her lap and was rapidly flipping the pages. A precarious stack of magazines a foot tall teetered on her tray table, next to a Coke bottle. She glanced up as Reilly and I entered, then resumed her reading.

"Jessica," Reilly said, his voice gentle. "I'm Detective Reilly with the Boca Police Department. This is my . . . associate, Harriet Horowitz. We need to talk to you."

"So talk," she said, not taking her eyes off the page.

"May I have this?" Reilly said, placing a hand on her magazine.

"No!" she pulled on it, glaring at us, her pupils wide and black.

"Okay," Reilly said. "Can we talk while you read?"

"Of course. You think I can't multitask? What do you think I am, a retard?"

"No, I don't think that, Jessica," Reilly said.

"Good. 'Cause I scored in the 99th percentile on the Florida standardized test." She reached for the Coke bottle and took a sip.

Reilly and I exchanged glances.

"Jessica Jarrett," Reilly said, "you're under arrest for the murder of Demarcus Pritchard."

Jessica kept reading as Reilly recited the Miranda rights. "Do you understand these rights as they have been stated to you?" Reilly concluded.

"Sure," the girl said, taking another sip.

"Jessica, your fingerprints were found on the weapon that killed Demarcus. Can you explain that for me?"

The girl's eyes looked up, her head remaining bent toward the page. She shifted her gaze from Reilly to me, then back to her reading. "I don't have to explain anything."

"No, you don't," Reilly agreed. "But you should know we also found your prints on the other half of the phone book that Demarcus was clutching. Which was hidden in an air vent in a restroom at The Oasis. All the evidence points to you as his killer."

The girl was silent as she turned a page.

"Jessica, you're going to remain here under police custody until you recover from your wound," Reilly said. "Then you'll go to juvie hall to await trial. After that, it's likely you'll go to prison for a long, long time."

The girl raised her eyes. They emitted a feverish glow. Her lips curved into a creepy smile.

"There's lots of books in prison, right? And newspapers? And magazines? I could spend the rest of my life in there doing nothing but . . . reading." A dreamy look crept into her gaze.

Reilly looked down at the floor. "No, Jessica. It doesn't work that way."

She banged a fist on the bed railing, shaking the frame and the IV pole she was hooked up to. "Okay, so what if I did stab him? He came after me first, trying to get that phone book and my Coke for himself. He attacked me—just like Amber did that night in the dining room. The hedge clippers were lying right there, and he lunged for them. I had to defend myself, so I grabbed them first before he could."

Reilly and I exchanged glances again. Maybe the girl was telling the truth. And if she wasn't, who could ever prove otherwise?

"Now leave me alone," she said. "I want to read."

Chapter 21

OUTSIDE JESSICA'S room, Reilly made a call to arrange for the release of Jacques Bertrand, the Haitian gardener who had been wrongfully arrested for Demarcus's murder. I guess that was a lawsuit coming. But it wasn't my problem.

Before we left the hospital, we stopped in to see Lars and Gitta. We found them both dozing, Lars in his hospital bed and Gitta in a reclining chair beside him, holding his hand. Gitta was a sleeping beauty. Her long blonde hair flowed around her perfectly oval face, her lush lashes brushed her creamy cheeks, and her rosy lips parted slightly to reveal her gleaming white teeth.

Reilly perched on the edge of the recliner, took her other hand, and kissed her forehead. Gitta stirred awake. "Kevin," she said, her voice warm and husky. Evidently, he was her Prince Charming. Her eyes fluttered to me. "Harriet. Thank you for everything. Lars is going to be okay. He'll be discharged in the morning."

"Don't thank me," I said. "He wouldn't be here in the first place if it wasn't for me."

"Don't blame yourself, sweetie," Gitta said. "I'm his mother. I have ultimate responsibility." Wow. That was a radical personality transformation. Not that it helped assuage my guilt any.

"Honey," Reilly said to Gitta, "we . . . that is, Harriet and I . . . have identified Demarcus's killer and figured out what happened to the other adolescents who died. There will be no more attacks or deaths at The Oasis."

"Thank God," Gitta said. "But I'm not going back. I need to be with my children. But I will complete my treatment. As an outpatient. I'll do it for myself, for my family, and for you, Kevin." She sent him an adoring look.

I felt like a third wheel. "Well, I'll leave you two lovebirds."

Reilly cleared his throat. "Um, wait, Harriet. Uh, Gitta and I will always have the warmest gratitude toward you for uniting us."

"I'm hardly a matchmaker, Reilly." I mean, it was Gitta's last husband's murder that had united them. Jeez. I had no desire to be part of their fairy tale or their comedy of manners or whatever the hell it was. I mean, I had my own tale—as a crime-fighter, not a cupid.

As I turned to go, Lars stirred in the bed and opened his eyes. Seeing me, he sat up in bed, suddenly alert. "Miss H., Detective Reilly. Did you get Ms. LaFleur?"

"Yes, we got her, son," Reilly said. "The kids are safe from her now. Thanks to your sharp eyes and quick thinking."

"Yesss!" Lars pumped a fist in the air. "I like this PI stuff. What do you say, Miss H.—can I be your apprentice?" Glancing quickly at his mom, he added, "During my breaks from MIT, that is."

Great. Just great. I needed a teenage sidekick like I needed a sidecar on the Harley.

"I'll think about it," I said. But somehow I had a feeling that Lars's apprenticeship was inevitable.

I PULLED OUT of the hospital parking lot and twisted the throttle to speed up. At long last, I was free. I coasted through Boca's deserted early-morning streets, my body and mind humming in tune with my Hog.

I longed for only one thing—Lior.

He lived in an apartment above his martial arts studio, and I headed there. But I found the place locked up, and there was no response to my ringing the doorbell. Maybe he was fast asleep. After all, he had flown in from Israel, then been nearly killed, then hospitalized. He had to be exhausted.

So was I. It was time for me to go to my home. My log cabin in the Glades.

I mounted my bike again and rode to the edge of land, where my airboat waited for me in the swamp. I unlatched and pulled out the boat's ramp, rolled the bike onto the boat, and secured it with its tie-downs. After I inserted my earplugs and topped them with my noise-cancelling headphones, I turned the engine. The huge rear-mounted fan started its frenzied spin. I shifted into gear and took off, skimming the surface of the shimmering water.

The sun was just rising behind me as I headed northwest. It cast a peach glow across this river of grass that I called home. A short-tailed hawk soared overhead, and a pair of Florida redbelly turtles floated by.

As I rounded a curve around a cypress island, I spotted something atop a half-submerged log. Could it be . . . A long, ridged back. A tail dipping into the water. Glistening eyeballs gazing skyward, as if contemplating the meaning of life.

It was! Lana.

Awww—she'd come out to greet me.

I cut the engine and removed my ear protection. The boat bobbed silently in the slow-moving stream.

Hey, I said.

Hey, she replied. *Everything good?*

Everything's good. I met your great-nephew, Slick.

How's that boy doin'? He stayin' out of trouble?

Yeah, he's a good kid.

Glad to hear it. Now give it up, girl! What happened at that addiction place?

I sighed. I was exhausted, but I knew I really couldn't put the case behind me until I processed it with Lana—the voice of my conscience. So I laid out the whole sorry story for her.

Mmm-mmm-mmm, she said when I finished. If she could have shaken her head, she would have, but her neck was too thick.

So Jessica may never be charged in the death of Demarcus, Lana said.

That's right. She claims it was self-defense, and who's to say otherwise? Demarcus isn't talking.

That poor girl was both a victim and a perpetrator, Lana said.

So was Demarcus, perhaps, and Amber, the girl who in turn stabbed Jillian. It's an all too common circumstance in the annals of crime, I said.

We floated in silence for a while.

Reilly told me Demarcus's funeral is tomorrow, I said. *I'll be going.*

I avoid cemeteries. Folks seem to get all discombobulated if I make an appearance. But I'll be thinking of him.

In the distance, a woodpecker tapped at a tree trunk.

The sun was higher on the horizon now, and a soft breeze rustled the swamp reeds.

Prison's not good enough for Gardenia for what she did to those kids, Lana said. *Why don't you get her out here, and I'll take care of her?*

It was a tempting offer. *No, not this time,* I said. *You know, I believe her when she said she never meant to hurt the kids. In her twisted way, she thought she was helping. And I can kind of see how she thought that. I mean, what about the rich kids that Lars told me about, who use performance-enhancing drugs to improve their academic performance? It's just another way the powerful maintain their privilege. And who's stopping them?*

I hear you, sister. But Gardenia did hurt "her kids." And she's gotta answer for her actions.

Of course. And she will. Though it may not be the way we'd like it.

I think that woman herself became addicted. To success. She couldn't stop herself even when she knew she was harming the kids.

You could be right, I said.

Hey—what about that Shrimp Pimp? What are you gonna do about her?

I'll rat her out. There's another victim-slash-perp for you. She needs help. But at the same time she's pimping minors. Or trying to, anyway. That's about as low as it gets.

And Stillwater?

I don't know, Lana. The fact is, she's actually a good doctor, I think. She has knowledge and empathy. She is helping people.

And maybe harming a few celebrities along the way. Where do you draw the line?

Damn her, she always asked the hard questions. And I didn't always have the answers. Like now. So I didn't say anything.

I guess Lana got the message, because she changed the subject.

So, what was it like being clean and sober for a couple days?

Awful. You know what? I did miss my Hennessy. I was starting to worry I'd have to give that up. But once I got out of there and onto my Hog, I realized that's the only thing that really makes me high. And I'll never relinquish that freedom and power.

An ibis glided over and landed on the log next to Lana. Did it realize it was taking its life in its hands? Or putting it in her jaws, rather? Nature was cruel. I wasn't going to change that. Avenging human cruelty was the best I could do.

You know what else I realized I missed while I was in that place? I said.

Me? Lana pulled back a lip. Either that was a grin or a preparation to snap at the bird. I guess the bird thought the latter, as it spread its wings and flapped away, safe for another day.

Yeah, you, I admitted. *And the rest of my self-assembled family. Lior. Enrique and Chuck. The Contessa. Lupe. I used to consider myself a loner. Now I realize I need them. And that's okay.*

And what about your biological family—your mother? And her man— Leonard.

Shit. I'd forgotten about them. Jeez, what a jerk I was, rhapsodizing about my friends while ignoring the other important people in my life. Especially after Leonard had served as my lifeline to the outside world when I'd first checked into The Oasis, and then come through with that liquid analysis gizmo. I'd call them ASAP. But I still didn't have my phone—I hadn't gone back to The Oasis to retrieve it. Right now, I just needed to collapse and sleep.

Come on, I said to Lana. *Let's go home.*

She slithered off the log into the water and paddled her feet to propel herself.

I donned my headgear, restarted the engine, and reoriented the boat. Up ahead—right in the direction of my cabin—there was a strange glow of light bursting through the breaking dawn. Red and orange and yellow.

What the hell? Was my cabin on fire?

I pulled on the throttle and practically flew across the water, Lana paddling like mad in my wake. The tall sawgrass obscured my view, letting only the eerie glow through.

When I was ten feet away, I could finally see the cabin.

It was no fire. It was a line of electric lights strung across my front porch. In huge letters, the lights spelled out, "Happy Birthday."

My fortieth. Today. I'd forgotten all about it.

A sleek yellow kayak bobbed at the side of the cabin, tied to the porch. And Lior sat in the rocking chair on that porch. His chest and biceps strained against his tight black T-shirt. His long, jeans-clad legs stretched before him. The reflection of the lights glistened off his jet-black hair and his chocolate-brown eyes.

He stood as I pulled up the boat and cut the engine. When I took off my headphones and earplugs, he stretched out his arms.

"Welcome home, baby," he said.

Suddenly I felt a surge of energy. My exhaustion disappeared.

I walked off the boat, into his arms, and into the next decade of my life.

The End

Acknowledgments

Hugs and kisses to Team Harriet: Pat Van Wie, Deborah Smith, Debra Dixon, and Danielle Childers of BelleBooks / Bell Bridge Books and Paige Wheeler of Creative Media Agency. And more to my invaluable critique group: Christine Jackson, Kristy Montee, Neil Plakcy, and Sharon Potts. And to Karen Dodge, whose dedicated career in substance abuse treatment has provided fodder for the fictional world depicted herein.

About the Author

Miriam Auerbach is the author of a satirical mystery series set in Boca Raton, Florida and featuring Harley-riding, wisecracking female private eye Harriet Horowitz. Her debut novel, Dirty Harriet, won the Romantic Times Reviewers' Choice Award for Best First Series Romance. Miriam can only assume that this is because the heroine kills her husband on page one. In a parallel universe, Miriam is known as Miriam Potocky, professor of social work at Florida International University in Miami. She lives in South Florida with her husband and their multicultural canines, a Welsh Corgi and a Brussels Griffon.

Visit Miriam at miriamauerbach.com.

or

Facebook at AuthorMiriamAuerbach

CPSIA information can be obtained at www.ICGtesting.com
Printed in the USA
LVOW12s2126300115

425118LV00002B/110/P